PENGUIN BOOKS

4 PAX TO EMPTINESS

Stella Kon's best-known work is the monodrama *Emily of Emerald Hill*, which appeared in 1982 and has since been performed almost a thousand times in Singapore, Malaysia and elsewhere. She has also written poems, novels and other plays, and librettos for several musicals with composer Desmond Moey. In 2006 she helped to found the arts charity Musical Theatre Ltd, and was its chairperson for fourteen years. More about Stella can be found on her website, www.emilyofemeraldhill.com.sg.

Stella loves to travel to visit her two sons and their families—Mark, Colette and children in Harrogate, Yorkshire, and Luke and Gini and children in Sydney, Australia. She meditates regularly with the Singapore branch of the World Community for Christian Meditation.

Plays by Stella Kon: *The Bridge, Trial, Emily of Emerald Hill, Dragon's Teeth Gate.*

Collections: 9 *Classroom Plays, 3 Stellar Plays.*

Novels: *The Scholar and the Dragon, Eston.*

Musicals: *Lost in Transit, Peter and Pierre, Merlion, Emily the Musical, Lim Boon Keng the Musical.*

Four Pax To Emptiness

Stella Kon

PENGUIN BOOKS

An imprint of Penguin Random House

PENGUIN BOOKS

USA | Canada | UK | Ireland | Australia
New Zealand | India | South Africa | China | Southeast Asia

Penguin Books is part of the Penguin Random House group of companies
whose addresses can be found at global.penguinrandomhouse.com

Published by Penguin Random House SEA Pvt. Ltd
9, Changi South Street 3, Level 08-01,
Singapore 486361

Penguin
Random House
SEA

First published in Penguin Books by Penguin Random House SEA 2023
Copyright © Stella Kon 2023

ISBN 9789815058949

Typeset in Garamond by MAP Systems, Bangalore, India
Printed at Markono Print Media Pte Ltd, Singapore

www.penguin.sg

Contents

BOOK ONE

Dongshandu

Chapter One

The four passengers from Singapore walked into the airport building at Dongshandu. It was their first touchdown in mainland China. They were twelve hours' flying time from home.

For the first five hours out from Changi International, they had not really left Singapore's mental airspace. Cocooned in the glistening efficiency of SIA's cabin service, they had still been in a familiar climate. Then they had passed through the frenetic bustle of Hong Kong's Chek Lap Kok, their passports were stamped, and they had entered the People's Republic of China.

They boarded a China Airlines flight, seven hours to this regional airport in central China. On the flight, looking at the food and the cabin decor and the other passengers, they began to know they were in a country whose ways of doing things were different from their own. They felt the decrease in opulence, the less-assiduous attention to their comfort and gratification.

As they approached Dongshandu, they looked down and saw a spreading brown plain, and a distant horizon, partly shrouded in blowing dust. Below, a grey urban sprawl, to which the plane was ear-poppingly descending. Modern factories belching smoke and flat-roofed apartment blocks. Miles of grey roofs with up-tilted corners: old houses, stretching into the distance, stretching back into the past, reminding the Singaporeans that people had lived here for incomprehensible generations on generations. And beyond the immediate horizon, the brown fields and hills stretched on endlessly in the hugeness of a strange country.

They stepped off the plane into the cold of a northern November. They looked for their baggage. Two workers hauled in a trolley piled high with bags which were dumped onto the floor. They found their possessions and headed for the main hall of the terminal building.

Katrina came first, walking fast in her Reeboks and designer jeans—a young executive away from the office, with things to do and people to see. Then came Lumy, Mrs Lumiere Chan, in black stretch pants and a printed silk blouse, with diamond rings on her fingers with maroon-lacquered nails; the wrinkles on those hands showed her age of sixty-two, which was not evident in her smooth, well-cosmeticized face.

Behind the two women, Alex pushed Peter's wheelchair. Alex, solid and practical-looking, ran his own construction-materials company. Peter was a paraplegic, dark and thin and intense, leaning forwards in the chair as though to direct his way by force of will.

They reached ten steps that led up to the main hall of the airport. Katrina halted her brisk stride and waited for the chair to catch up. She stooped lithely to grab one footrest of the chair while Lumy bent to take the other. Peter threw his weight back in the chair as Alex tipped it backward and lifted. Smoothly, the three carried the wheelchair up the steps and set it down in the main hall, under the sign that bore the name Dongshandu Regional Airport.

So, the four from Singapore came to this place: the executive, the *tai-tai*, the cripple and the businessman, drawn by a common goal to an unlikely destination, on a mission to save the world. With them came Bezalia, unseen fifth to their party, divine hitchhiker on their souls.

They looked around the crowded arrival hall. It struck them as dingy and comfortless. It was a large hall with a cement floor. The walls were covered with green paint which was peeling off here and there. There were faded airline posters and ranks of uncushioned wooden benches. If there was heating, they could not feel it. Four television screens poured out sound.

The place was full of people elbowing each other at the checkout desks, yelling in Putonghua with an accent that the Singaporeans could barely understand. They crowded the benches, they sat on the floor along the walls, with their bundles and bags at their feet. All those nearby gazed at the foreigners with wide curious stares.

'Okay, let's check in for the Zhengzhou flight,' Katrina said briskly, hardly noticing that she had taken charge of her friends. 'Where's Pei Tong Air?' She looked around, above the crowd, and saw a white signboard with blue Chinese and English characters. 'There it is, Pei Tong Air, give me your tickets, I'll get us checked in.'

'There's nobody there,' said Alex, peering through the crowd. The counter below the sign was deserted. 'They aren't open.'

'Not open?' Katrina said disbelievingly and forced her way across to stare at the empty counter. She stood baffled, a get-things-done person who couldn't do anything, feeling paralysing weakness in her knees, emptiness in her gut.

Bezalia! She cried in her mind, a silent scream of protest and fear.

It's okay. No need to fall apart, came a calm voice in her head.

I can't do anything! I'm helpless!

Being powerless is not going to kill you dead. Katrina heard Bezalia's gentle mockery in her mind, feeling the warmth of her smile. *Accept it. Allow it to be.* All this in a brief moment, while Katrina stood flat-footed and slack-jawed at the empty airlines counter.

Then she rubbed her cheeks briskly and turned to the next busy counter and asked questions of the woman there. She went back to her friends.

'The counter won't open at till afternoon,' Katrina reported to the others. 'She couldn't say exactly when. The flight to

Zhengzhou is at five p.m. so maybe they'll open at around three, huh? We'll just have to wait.'

'Okay. It's eleven now—shall we get something to eat?' Alex suggested.

Lumy said, 'I need to go to the toilet.'

Katrina laughed. 'Now we're going to know—whether everything they said about China toilets is true or not!'

'I see some food stalls over there,' Alex said, as the women departed. 'I heard in northern China they eat a lot of wheat buns, *mandou*. Peter, you look after our bags, I'll see what I can find . . .'

'No, I don't think so,' said Peter calmly. 'If somebody takes our stuff while you're away, I won't be able to do anything about it.'

'You could yell and attract people's attention . . .'

'They might not help.'

Alex blinked. His mind boggled at the picture of somebody walking up and robbing a crippled man; of Peter yelling at the thief to stop, and all those onlookers sitting still and doing nothing to help. 'Bloody bastards here no damn use,' he began to swear furiously. The small boy who lived inside his competent exterior felt the threatening alienness of their situation, their isolation from friendly help, and began to thrash around in rage.

It's okay, Alex, came the soothing voice in his mind. He felt unseen arms go around him, to hold him in a firm and reassuring embrace. He let out a breath slowly and sat down again.

'Okay, better wait till the women come back. And then you and I can go to the gents', and then we can look for something to eat.'

The women came back. 'Terrible! Terrible!' They waved their hands and rolled their eyes as they described the toilets.

'Lucky, I have my urinal,' Peter said smugly. 'Alex just has to empty it for me and rinse it out.'

'If the men's toilet has a tap with running water,' Katrina said sardonically.

Alex wheeled Peter's chair towards the male toilets. The women stood beside their pile of luggage, looking around the crowded hall. The people nearby had stared at the wheelchair and Peter's dark Indian features. But they stared just as hard at Katrina and Lumy and Alex: Singaporean Chinese whose racial traits were no different from those of the locals, but who in dress and speech and manner came from a different world.

Katrina, gazing around, saw among the faded travel posters on the wall, one that was newer than the others. It showed a temple in northern China, on whose facade was an image that Katrina knew well. 'Look,' she whispered to Lumy, pointing, 'Look at that!'

A white-robed goddess stood on the brow of a dragon as it plunged through a stormy sea, dark tumult around her. The white robes of the goddess did not flutter in the gale. She was the still centre of the tempest, the light at the heart of the storm.

'Lady of the Winds,' Katrina whispered.

'Your picture—of Bezalia,' Lumy said.

Katrina had found the same image in a temple in Singapore. Now she found it again in this alien place, like a welcoming friend. It was the only new poster there and looked as though it had been put up that morning. Light radiated from the slim figure. Her face was calm and full of stern compassion. Her eyes were half-closed, as though she had seen and understood all the suffering of the world.

Thank you, Katrina said internally.

'I need to sit down,' Lumy said.

There were no empty seats in the hall. The wooden benches had been made to accommodate four people. A few benches were occupied by a single person each, stretched out full-length and sleeping; on other benches sat two or three people, with bundles and bags stacked in the space beside them. Around the benches, groups of travellers sat cross-legged on the dirty floor, or leaned against the walls.

'Look,' said Lumy. 'Over there, that group of people is getting up!' She and Katrina gathered the many bags. 'Quickly, quickly!' They moved laboriously towards the place where a couple of benches were being vacated.

'Oh shit,' Katrina said. As they approached the benches, another family slid into the vacant seats. They settled themselves in place, talking loudly together. They ignored Katrina and Lumy who stood nearby, panting and frustrated, their luggage scattered around them. It was being ignored, Katrina thought, that was more infuriating than losing the place; it was the way the local family acted as though they did not see the foreigners at whom everyone else was staring.

The men came back, Peter holding a couple of paper bags. 'There's no restaurant. We got some of those mandou,' Alex said.

'We tried to sit down,' Katrina said, 'But other people got in first.'

'Next time we have to be very fast,' Lumy planned. 'Look carefully. Wait till we see more people getting ready to move. More people will be moving. The next plane is going to depart. Katrina and I must go first and take the places. There! Some people are getting up!'

Katrina and Lumy pushed hastily to where another group was gathering their possessions. They stood as near as they could to the bench, so that they could sit down on the seats the instant they were vacated. Meanwhile, Alex began to bring their luggage and Peter rolled himself towards them.

Lumy sat down at one end of the bench. Katrina sat in the middle. A large woman, her arms full of bundles, lowered herself into the space between them. Almost instinctively, Katrina began to move aside to make room for her. But Lumy scooted up closer so that she was next to Katrina, and the descending woman found herself almost sitting on Lumy's lap. She straightened up. Without turning round or looking at Lumy, she set her leg, clad in a blue trouser and shod with a cheap tennis shoe, against Lumy's leg and she shoved to push Lumy out of the way.

Katrina felt her heart pounding and her adrenaline pumping like when she played tennis. As Lumy was shoved down the bench, Katrina slid down beside her so that the intruding woman still could not sit down. At the same time, Katrina dumped her shoulder bag on the far end of the bench so that no one could sit down on that empty space.

She looked up—glared, rather—at the woman, who looked back at her with emotionless stolidity. With her was a man in a purple nylon jacket. Alex had come up with the bags, and he tried to sit on the end of the bench where Katrina had placed her shoulder-bag. The man in the purple jacket moved close and blocked Alex's way. He put his hand on Katrina's bag as though to remove it; Katrina pressed it down on the seat.

Peter arrived. He rolled himself up in his chair and made the rubberized footrest nudge hard into the man's leg. The locals turned round and saw the wheelchair with its blue canvas seat and its gleaming chromium frame; and in it, the thin man with his brown face and high sharp nose and large bright eyes, wearing a red ski-jacket.

While they stared at this apparition, Peter spoke some of his few Chinese words. 'Hey, friend!' he said and held out two white buns from the paper bag. He smiled broadly and pressed them into the hands of the man in the purple jacket. 'Friend,' he said again to the woman and held out more buns towards her.

The stolid expression on the woman's face broke up. In a moment of confusion, the look that did not see them as people, only as obstacles to her way, disappeared, then she smiled. She pushed out her hands to refuse the buns in traditional motions of courtesy. Peter beamed and nodded and pressed the buns on her. She and her male companion accepted them. Their thrusting force had disappeared. Meanwhile, Alex had sat down on the end of the bench.

'Where do you come from?' the Chinese woman asked, eating the bun as she stood in front of them.

'From Singapore,' replied Alex, who spoke Putonghua best from the travellers.

'Taiwan,' the woman said beaming.

'Singapore,' Alex repeated. The woman spoke a flood of words, but he could not understand her accent.

'She said America,' Katrina said. 'I think she's talking about Taiwan and America . . . political stuff.'

'Ask her about the village of Chengshen,' Lumy said. Alex and Katrina did so. Communication was difficult. The woman had no experience in talking to people who did not understand her language. She did not know how to slow her words down or to speak more simply, she just spoke louder as to the deaf. 'Yes, yes! You can go! Chengshen is very nice, you will get there very easily!' she said. Her husband said the same thing, loud and jovial.

Meanwhile, Lumy had arranged their luggage around the bench, defining a kind of space for themselves in the hall. Alex and Katrina and Lumy sat on the bench, Peter in his wheelchair facing them. The couple stood near them and talked. Peter smiled and spoke in English to the couple and Alex translated what he said. Katrina struggled to understand and to converse. She thought the pair were completely ignorant, knowing nothing of the village of Chengshen or how to get there.

While they talked, they ate the remainder of the buns. 'A bit rough,' said Lumy. 'At home, Peking Restaurant makes mandou, very soft and smooth, better than these ones!'

'All right,' Peter said when they had finished eating. 'Let's do Listening.' Lumy nodded. Katrina and Alex looked at him doubtfully.

'Here?' said Katrina. 'Maybe we could wait till we get to a hotel?'

'Maybe we should do it now, while we have time.' Peter overruled her gently. 'It was twelve hours ago that we did it at Changi.'

'I didn't mind at Changi,' Katrina muttered, thinking that it was less frightening to behave oddly when they were on home ground than here, where they were surrounded by strangers.

Peter smiled at the couple and said to Alex, 'Ask them to excuse us for a while.'

'What do I tell them?'

'Just say we are going to meditate. I think they can understand that.'

'I don't know how to say "meditation!"'

'Oh . . . well, tell them we are going to pray. Ask them to help keep an eye on our bags!' The couple withdrew a little away and continued to watch with interest.

'I've got the timer,' said Alex, pressing buttons on his watch.

They settled themselves; Alex and Lumy setting their backs upright against the back of the bench, Katrina drawing up her legs to cross them in a lotus position. They closed their eyes. Peter sat upright in his wheelchair, hands resting on his thighs, his breath already slowing and deepening.

'Listen to stillness. Listen to silence,' he said softly. 'Listen to the voice of your heart.'

The four sat motionless and listened. Around them was the hubbub of the airport, noisy conversations which they couldn't understand. Voices rising and falling. Clatter and crashing, somewhere in the hall. They listened, let the sounds wash over them, unidentified and unanalysed. Presently, these noises seemed to recede, to be coming from a distance. Nearby was the throb of their own hearts beating, and the slow tide of breath going in and out.

They listened. They stayed in that silent place as best they could. Stray thoughts floated in and out.

Katrina found her mind running on flight schedules and travel bookings. She kept catching herself back, and starting anew to listen, to ignore the incessant rattle of thought, to try to find the silent place. Alex started thinking about Cynthia. He was seven minutes into unhappy fretting about her, before he recalled himself and started trying to listen again, to let go of worrying and be still.

For Lumy, the entry to silence was almost immediate. She ceased hearing the noises of the airport hall. She heard the sounds of her own heart and breath. Then these too became distant and remote, and she felt a friend with her, like an arm around her shoulders, like a warm cheek against her own.

Bezalia, she said in her mind, and smiled. Then, not holding to that happiness, she sank deeper and deeper into silence and stillness. She came to a place where she could not move or think. She lost awareness of herself; she was aware of nothing. She rested, in darkness and peace.

Peter spent the thirty minutes in attentive listening. With the discipline of long practice, he focused on his heartbeat and his breathing. He was aware of no presence, no special joy. He sat still, and when the timer went off, he stretched his shoulders and smiled contentedly.

Chapter Two

The journey to China had begun six weeks earlier, with Peter rolling his wheelchair into the office of a banker in a Shenton Way tower.

'Hey, Peter, how are you, how was the Kinabalu trip?'

'The boys have made a set of photos for you,' said Peter. He took papers from his zip case and handed over a small photograph album.

The banker leafed through it with interest. He looked at pictures of sturdy climbers hauling two reinforced wheelchairs up steep slopes. Eight expedition members stood posing on the mountain summit, with glowing faces full of good fellowship. They carried a banner naming the bank as the sponsor of the Kinabalu expedition of the Singapore Society for the Disabled.

'You mean your guys really carried the wheelchair chaps all the way up Mount Kinabalu!'

'Not all the way, Eric! Those paraplegics could manage themselves on the ropes and haul themselves up or down.'

Eric looked at the photos and marvelled. 'It's great that those poor guys can go to the top of the mountain,' he said. 'They don't let their handicap stop them from seeing the world, huh? It is really a good cause for the bank to support. A good cause,' he repeated, having had to justify to his masters the allocation of resources to a project so seemingly unproductive as mountain-climbing by the physically handicapped. He did not know how to explain, even to himself, that his own heart had been unaccountably lifted, by having contributed to a victory of the human spirit over adversity.

'So, Peter, what can I do for you today?'

'I want to go to China,' Peter told the banker.

'Which part of China? Is it for the SSD?'

'I want to go to a town called Chengshen, in Henan province. It's not for SSD, it's a project of my own. It is very important, at a global level.' Peter paused. 'Do you have time to listen? This might take a while to explain.'

'Yes, yes, I have time,' Eric said. He liked talking to Peter. He liked the genial, philanthropic side of himself which emerged in Peter's company. 'Tell you what, let's go for lunch and talk it over!'

'Eric, this is not something you want to hear over lunch,' Peter said. 'Tell me something: how Chinese do you consider yourself?' Eric Lee, who belonged to one of Singapore's oldest and wealthiest families, smiled and shook his head. 'My grandfather's grandfather came from China more than a hundred years ago. We have lost touch with any kinfolk there. We look Chinese but we don't relate much to the culture, we're very Westernized. I suppose we are something like you educated Indians, Peter!'

Peter smiled, hearing the racial condescension of which Eric was entirely unaware. 'But you still think of yourself as pure-blooded Chinese, don't you? How close do you feel to the people of the PRC?'

'Not at all,' said Eric. 'Frankly, the PRC people seem to regard us overseas Chinese either as barbarians who deserted the mother country, or as gold mines to be exploited. I could tell you stories! Anyway, what's all this about?'

'Have you ever heard about the big famine in China, during the time of Mao Tse Tung's Great Leap Forward? Around 1958–62?'

'Before the Cultural Revolution? I know they did have a bad famine then. There were floods and natural disasters and the crops failed. Lots of people died.'

'Do you know any details?'

'No, I was only a kid. I remember seeing our *amah* packing cardboard boxes, to send to her relatives. My mother gave her old clothes. And she sent food parcels, preserved duck and sausages, I imagined the children in China eating these delicacies every day.'

'So, you knew that there was starvation in China. And you have heard that the famine was due to crop failure. But during those years China was exporting grain. They donated free grain to Albania and North Korea.'

Eric frowned. 'What do you mean? What are you getting at?'

'The famine was not a natural occurrence. The low harvests were due to Mao's disastrous farming policies. Starvation happened because the government seized food stocks from the peasants. Throughout the famine, the state granaries were full of grain, and China was exporting grain and pork and poultry. Meanwhile, throughout the country, there wasn't enough to eat.'

'That sounds crazy,' Eric protested.

'Yes, it was crazy. Lunacy on a scale you can't imagine. How many people do you think died in this famine? Just make a guess.'

'My god,' Eric said, frowning as he tried to force his mind into unpleasant channels. 'China's total population in the 1950s was, what, half a billion? China is like India, isn't it, the numbers are so big you have to double every estimate . . . I think I read that in the old days people died by tens of thousands, even hundreds of thousands. I can see from your signals that the figure is much bigger, so I will multiply by ten. A few million maybe? Over three years . . . maybe three or four million, is that about the right size of figure?'

'Three million, as big as Singapore's whole population,' Peter said unsmiling. 'In North Korea this year, two million have starved to death. China is a lot bigger than North Korea.' Peter touched the papers in front of him. 'Various authorities give different figures. The best, middle-of-the-range estimate, is that about thirty million people died in the famine.'

Eric stared. 'Thirty million!'

'The Jewish Holocaust was six million deaths. The number who died under Stalin was estimated at twelve million. Thirty million people died in China, between 1958 and 1962.'

'Thirty million,' Eric repeated, bemusedly. 'It's incredible. You're telling me that Mao deliberately starved thirty million people to death?'

'No, I didn't say it was deliberate. Mao made the famine. But he did not do it by intention. He didn't know, or he pretended not to know, or he believed he didn't know that he was causing it.'

Eric had never seen such a bleak look on Peter's face or heard such quiet anger in his voice. He told Eric a tale that would have the banker lying awake at night, trying to grasp the horror and enormity of what he had heard. He would never have believed it, even from Peter, except for the pile of photocopies of evidence from various sources.

'You've heard the story of the Emperor's New Clothes? It was just like that. There was a lie that there was plenty of food in China. Mao believed it, and all his followers helped him to believe the lie. Nobody dared to tell the truth . . . to say that the people were starving, that the emperor had no clothes.'

Peter went on in bitter, even tones. 'The first lie was to say that in 1958, China had harvests incredibly bigger than anything ever seen before. It was the first year of Mao's Great Leap Forward. He enforced various new agricultural methods, based on crackpot science. To report that these methods failed, was considered treason to the Great Helmsman. His followers reported fantastic improvements in agriculture that year; fields yielding harvests ten or twelve times greater than the harvests of traditional methods. And since the harvest figures were so big, the tax that the government took was correspondingly increased. The usual tax was around thirty per cent.'

Peter picked up a page of notes. 'Here are some typical figures. In a certain county in Henan province, the actual harvest was about 88,000 tonnes, but the cadres zealously reported 239,000 tonnes. Eric, what happens if you tax thirty per cent of the inflated figure?'

'Your tax is 71,700 tonnes,' Eric said after a moment. 'But that's nearly eighty percent of the actual harvest!'

'So, there was a gap between the reported figures, which showed huge surpluses of grain, and what was actually available on the ground. The second big lie was that the gap was because the peasants were holding back grain and concealing it from the tax collectors. They were called enemies of the people. Many millions of peasants were killed and tortured for that crime.

'Meanwhile, the whole country was starving. But no one in authority dared to admit that this was happening. From the lowest village officials to the ministers surrounding Mao himself, people who spoke of food shortages were treated as traitors, punished, or executed. That was the third big lie. In 1960, the President of China, Liu Shaoqi, visited Henan province. The hungry peasants had stripped bark from roadside trees to eat. Local party officials plastered the trees with clay and straw to hide the damage, to try to conceal the truth from the President.

'Liu Shaoqi realized the people were starving. Eventually, he pushed through his reforms to reverse Mao's disastrous policies. By 1963, the famine was over, and Mao's political position was under threat. In 1966, he launched the Cultural Revolution, to regain his power.'

'I can't believe it,' Eric muttered. 'We've never heard of this terrible famine!'

'The lie continues, Eric. The silence was never broken. To this day, the Chinese government does not openly admit how many people died, or that Mao was to blame. The culture of the suppression of truth continues, destroying China's soul.'

Eric moved his hands helplessly, grasping for meaning. 'It's terrible,' Eric sighed. 'But what does it have to do with you? It was thirty years ago! Why are you going to China?'

'I want to go to a village called Chengshen, in Henan province. The whole village starved to death. The people were not buried, they lay in their huts or where they fell by the roadside. I want to go to where the famine was worst and find the field where many bodies lay and light candles on those unmarked graves.'

Eric looked at him in bewilderment.

'It was a terrible thing that happened,' Peter said calmly. 'I want to do something to mourn for that disaster. Not only on my behalf . . . but for the sake of all people everywhere. I want to help to heal the world.'

'Oh . . . Ah,' said Eric. Under Peter's intense, dark gaze, he felt mystified and inadequate. Anyone else producing these feelings in him would have been ushered out of his office minutes ago. 'So how can I help you, Peter? You want airfares to go to China? How many people in your party?'

'I can get some help from Chan Leong Holdings—'

'Oh, you've got Chan Leong in on it!' Eric said in some relief. His mind poked once more at the idea that Peter wanted to fly thousands of miles to light candles in some field in China and decided not to examine it any closer. 'I'll see what I can do. A trip to China—a cultural exchange—I can swing it. A lot of the directors do have their family and business connections there, they are the ones with roots in China.'

Peter rolled his chair out of Eric's office with Eric's agreement to help. Eric was still puzzled about why Peter wanted to go. This was not surprising. Peter had told Eric far less than everything about why he wanted to go, and why he wanted the bank to be involved.

Chapter Three

At half-past three, as the grey winter afternoon was fading beyond the grimy windows, two clerks switched on lights at the counter of Peidong Air, and a crowd gathered. Katrina hurried there, clutching a handful of plane tickets. She waited interminably, squeezed among odorous, jostling bodies. People pushed past her. She did some pushing of her own. At last, she was at the counter and laid her handful of tickets on the desk.

The clerk took the tickets and referred to his papers. 'No seats,' he said.

'What do you mean no seats?' Katrina cried. 'We have confirmed seats for Zhengzhou. Confirmed, okay.'

The clerk said something she couldn't catch. Katrina repeated herself, raising her voice. The clerk pointed to the tickets. 'Not okay.'

Katrina argued. She pointed to the 'OK' written on the tickets, the clerk shook his head. He waved her away and reached past her to the next person. Katrina pushed back to her friends. 'He says we have no seats! He says the seats were not confirmed!'

'But we confirmed them in Singapore!' Peter said. They looked at each other in frustration.

'He says we should have got them endorsed in Hong Kong. We needed to get another chop on the tickets.'

'The damn travel agent never told us,' Alex said, finding someone to blame.

'Never mind that. What can we do?' Peter asked. 'Can we get on the waitlist if there are any vacant seats?'

'I was trying to get him to waitlist us. Alex, you better come with me and talk to him. Make sure he puts us on the top of the list.'

Alex went back with Katrina to the counter, where the crowd seemed to have grown no smaller. It was now a quarter to five. Alex used his weight and strength to get to the front, and to demand the clerk's attention. 'Are there any empty seats? Can you put us on the wait list?'

'You wait.'

'How good are our chances? Do you think we can get seats?'

'Maybe there are seats. You wait.'

They waited. The crowd around the desk thinned as the passengers checked in and went towards the departure gates. At half-past five, the other clerk stood up from the counter and began to pack papers away.

'No seats,' the desk clerk said to Alex. Katrina and Alex stared at each other, realizing that their plane had departed.

'How do we get onto the next flight?' Katrina asked the clerk. He explained that they had to go to the airline office in the city, get their tickets endorsed, and book seats on the next evening's flight.

'Where are we going to sleep tonight! Can you tell us where we can stay? Can you give us the name of a hotel?'

'Daishan Hotel,' the clerk wrote on a scrap of paper.

Katrina and Alex went back to Lumy and Peter. 'We'll have to go to the city and check into this hotel for the night. In the morning we can go to the airline office. Let's go and look for a taxi to take us to town.'

'Be careful about the taxi,' Lumy said as they gathered their baggage and headed out of the airport hall. 'Make sure you bargain for the price before we get in.'

'Yeah, we won't let him cheat us,' Alex said. He waved away the ragged porter who wanted to take his bag. Thinking of tales he had been told about taxi-drivers in foreign lands, thinking of the treatment they had met in China so far, he felt mistrustful of anyone they might have to deal with; full of hostility and suspicion.

Outside the building was no neat line of taxis, no liveried officer to direct the queues of passengers. In the chill evening air, taxis and cars pulled to the kerb and people rushed for them. The first time that Alex hailed a taxi, someone else opened the back door and jumped into the cab while Alex was bending to talk to the driver through the front window. He stood there, open-mouthed, looking at his friends and their pile of baggage and Peter in his wheelchair, deciding to be really aggressive while grabbing the next cab.

A vehicle pulled in to the kerb, brakes squealing, clouds of brown smoke rising from the clattering exhaust pipe. A man leaned out to them. A red cloth was tied round his brow, his jaw was covered with white stubble. His eyes were black slits amidst merry wrinkles, his crooked yellow teeth showed in a wide grin. 'Taxi, come come come!' he cried hoarsely.

Alex thrust the piece of paper with the hotel's address into the man's face. 'Daishan Hotel—one hundred yuan!' he said loudly.

'One hundred yuan!' the man agreed, grinning cheerfully, and leaving the engine running he came down from the taxi, hurried around to his passengers, and began throwing their bags into the boot of the car. Lumy watched anxiously while Alex and Katrina got Peter into the front seat of the cab, with the wheelchair folded and stowed on top of the baggage in the boot. The driver jumped back behind the wheel. They drove off into the dimly lit streets of the town.

'Where do you come from?' the driver asked in the thick local accent.

'Singapore.'

'Singapore, eh? What business are you doing in Dongshandu?'

'We're trying to get to a place called Chengshen,' Katrina answered. She felt there was friendliness in the driver's questions, as well as curiosity.

'Ah! Are all of you going to Chengshen?'

'Yes, we're all going.'

The driver grinned at Peter. 'You're pretty good, huh! Your legs don't work, but you travel around with your friends!'

Alex translated and Peter said, 'Tell him, with my friends' help I can go anywhere in the world.'

'Why are you going to Daishan Hotel? It isn't good for you to go there!'

'Take us to Daishan Hotel,' Alex said sternly; suspicious again, afraid that they would be hijacked to some other destination.

'Yes, yes, Daishan Hotel! It is very expensive, but you overseas Chinese people like Daishan. That's where we will go.'

The taxi rattled onwards, between low buildings lining a narrow dusty road.

'I hope we can get adjacent rooms,' Katrina remarked to the others. 'We'd better check that the lift is wide enough to take the wheelchair, or perhaps we'd better try to stay on the ground floor. I'm dying to have a good hot bath. I presume a good hotel will have attached bathrooms.'

'And there should be a restaurant in the hotel,' Alex said.

Peter said, 'Tomorrow, we need to go to the airline office to sort out the tickets. Shall we ask this driver to fetch us in the morning?'

'Good idea,' Alex said. They had all begun to like this stranger, and to have a kind of trust in him. He made the request. 'Come and fetch us at the hotel at nine tomorrow, okay?'

'Very good, I'll come and get you,' the driver grinned cheerfully. 'My name is Loo. Old Loo, they call me!'

When they reached Daishan Hotel, Alex hurried into the bright, well-appointed lobby of the hotel. Katrina followed, to find him arguing with the receptionist.

'Now you listen to me,' he was saying. 'A big hotel like this, of course you have rooms. I will pay for them in US dollars!' He hauled out his wallet.

The clerk shook his head and said they had no vacancies.

'Look, maybe you have someone checking out tonight,' Alex said persuasively. 'Examine your records! I will wait for a while. This is my name, okay?' He pushed a folded paper across the desk.

Katrina pulled Alex away from the desk. 'Why should we wait around? If they are full, we'd better go look someplace else!'

'I gave the man ten dollars,' Alex said, with complacency that made Katrina want to slap him. 'Just give him ten minutes and he'll 'discover' he's got rooms for us!'

They went back to the taxi, where Lumy was telling Old Loo how to unfold the wheelchair. 'Better not unload our things,' Katrina said. 'We may not be able to get rooms here.'

'We'll get rooms,' Alex said confidently.

'What, no rooms here?' repeated Lumy, one step behind as usual. She wished the younger people wouldn't quarrel, and that they wouldn't talk so fast without explaining things properly.

'Just because you've got lots of money, doesn't mean you're bound to get rooms,' Katrina said to Alex, keeping her voice level.

'I tell you they like US dollars. I know what I'm doing,' growled Alex. He was irritated by Katrina's air of always knowing better than everyone else.

'We should ask them again. Maybe they have got extra rooms,' Lumy said. She went inside with Alex. Katrina stayed with Peter and talked to Old Loo, while Lumy and Alex went through all the motions Alex had gone through before; with a kind of stupid persistence, as though if you asked people the same question often enough, they'd eventually give you the answer you wanted.

Alex and Lumy came out. 'They say they don't have rooms!' said Lumy. 'Should we wait some more?'

'The driver knows another hotel,' Katrina interrupted, glad to have solved the problem. To her surprise, Alex temporized, saying they didn't know if the next place might be full also, and if they waited a bit longer the Daishan might find them rooms after all.

'Wait?' Katrina snapped. 'Perhaps you'd like to sit here all night, then you wouldn't need to worry about sleeping accommodation!'

'Let's go,' Peter said curtly. They piled into the taxi and Old Loo drove off again, with resentment and irritation simmering around them. Lumy gave a voluble account of the argument with the receptionist. Katrina and Alex ignored her. Peter was silent. His back was hurting fiercely after the long hours in the wheelchair, and his black leather case with the Percodan was with the other baggage in the boot.

At the next hotel—smaller and dingier—Old Loo jumped down from the taxi and hurried up to the reception desk. He talked earnestly to the desk clerk. There was shaking of heads. He spoke emphatically, and the desk clerk picked up the phone and made a couple of calls. Old Loo turned to Katrina and Alex, who had been standing on the side lines of his activity, and explained that this hotel was full, but he had secured them rooms in another hotel, eight miles away.

'Yeah, yeah, sure got rooms!' Alex sneered sarcastically. 'Should have waited in Daishan, right?' he said to Katrina, and 'Miss Smarty Pants,' added his tone of voice.

Katrina was furious. 'I don't think that would have been a good idea,' she said in the cool reasonable tone which she didn't know irritated Alex more than ever. She turned to Old Loo. 'Are there really rooms for us?'

'Really, really, I guarantee!'

They could only get back into the taxi, and rattle away again into the dark street.

Peter, in the front seat of the taxi, swallowed two pills without water and hoped they'd kick in soon. He could sense the simmering emotions in the back seat. He felt the crosscurrents of mutual animosity, as clearly as he heard the few sullen words they spoke.

My god, Bezalia, he thought, *this expedition is falling apart before it's begun! A fine leader I am, can't even get my team to the starting point without them snapping and tearing each other to pieces . . .*

A voice replied in his mind, warm and amused, *Did you think you were leading this expedition? Whatever gave you that idea?*

I got them into China. I made them come.

You had no power to make them do anything. They heard the same call you did, and they chose to answer it. A smile: *Hey, you aren't carrying the responsibility for this venture—does that make you feel any better?*

Yes, Ma'am!

Don't worry, Peter, said Bezalia. *You will be prepared for what you have to do.*

So, it's okay for them to grouse and bitch at each other?

It's not okay. But it's not your problem. Hang loose, Peter. Peter relaxed and half-dozed in the speeding car.

* * *

Katrina heard a friendly voice, pulling her out of an angry reverie. *What are you so mad about, Katrina?*

That Alex! Crass, blustering idiot, waving his money around . . .

Are you mad because he was stupid? Or because you looked bad too?

I was right! Of course I was!

Look at yourself. See yourself. Bezalia sent pictures to Katrina's inner eye, replaying the argument. Katrina winced as she saw herself, harsh and arrogant.

I'm not like that, Bezalia! I didn't raise my voice, I spoke politely!

What was in your heart? Bezalia said. Her words were a laser that laid bare Katrina's innermost thoughts and motives. Katrina saw her naked need to be superior; her compulsion to look better than anyone else around. She saw and was ashamed. She bit her lip in self-revulsion, for the ugly thing she knew herself to be.

Bezalia put an arm around her. Sitting in the taxi, Katrina felt the flow of comfort and reassurance like a physical sensation. *It's okay, my dear. You are as you are.* She knew the presence of love and grew calm in self-acceptance.

She said ruefully, *I messed up again! I still haven't learned to let go of that bitchy part of me.*

And the smiling answer came: *Don't worry! You have plenty of time to learn—you have your whole life in front of you!*

* * *

Alex seldom looked deep inside himself. His moods were like winds that blew over him, and he didn't know where they came from. As he sat fuming in the taxi, he heard the friendly greeting of the presence he had come to trust, since he encountered it five months ago, in the Sunday market at Marine Parade. He responded aggrievedly.

Yes, Bezalia, I'm sore at that snooty bitch Katrina!

You're sore at her, huh?

Yeah, yeah, I'm very fed-up with her! And the bloody China hotel also, wouldn't find a room for us! In the corners of his mind Alex had room for anger at Peter and Lumy too, for being unhelpful burdens.

Yes, Alex, you're mad at the whole wide world! Alex felt as though he was gently picked up in a pair of strong hands. The hands gave his mind a firm shake. He blinked, feeling the fog of anger drain away. *Do you still have anything to be angry about?* the voice inquired.

No, said Alex. The hands moved down his body in a repeated soothing motion, restoring him to calm. His jangled emotions returned to balance. By the time the taxi came to a halt, all trace of anger was gone. He jumped down and held out a hand to help Katrina alight. She took it, accepting his silent apology.

They unloaded their belongings with exhausted relief. It had been more than two hours since they had left the airport. They were cold and tired and hungry and resigned to paying exorbitantly for Loo's services.

'One hundred yuan!' Old Loo grinned. 'That's what we agreed at the beginning. Give me one hundred yuan, and tomorrow morning I will come back for you!' Alex paid, feeling pleased, but as though he'd tried to step on a step that wasn't there.

The hotel was small and shabby, but they were given two rooms, side by side on the lower floor. They got their wash, in communal showers at the end of the corridor, and a meal, which was noodles from a small shop around the corner.

At eleven at night, they gathered in the room Alex and Peter shared. They prepared to keep their regular appointment with the mystery of divinity.

'So tired!' Alex said. 'I think I cannot Listen tonight. Sure to fall asleep. I better not try to meditate.'

'Do it,' said Peter. 'Do it in respect for the daily task. Even if you fall asleep, or if your conscious mind is totally distracted, the work still goes on deep inside you.'

Peter said the opening words. They listened and heard the noises of the street, doors banging in the hotel, a television playing somewhere close by. After a while, there were soft snores from Alex.

Peter lay on the bed. His body was easier, but there was still tension in his mind. As he tried to listen, he seemed still to hear a hubbub of voices that called out and protested.

Images flickered past, disturbing him with echoes of anxiety and pain. A stony plain littered with white fragments of bone. Alex and his wife Cynthia, a hospital, a restaurant. A chequebook on a banker's desk. Blurred photographs in old newspapers. Faces like skulls, bony and hollow-eyed.

Peter was a man of much will-power, who had learned to combat the tyranny of self-will. He knew that this was the battle which was won by inaction, by not struggling. *Bezalia!* Peter said in his mind, *I can't do anything tonight!*

You're having trouble, aren't you? Stop dwelling on the past and looking to the future. Know that you are here, in this place, at this time.

I am here, Peter repeated.

I am with you, Bezalia said.

For that timeless moment, that was all that Peter needed.

* * *

As Katrina started listening, an image came to her mind, of a picture in a temple, in a street in Singapore. She had seen it one day, passing by, and her heart had said, *That is Bezalia.*

A goddess poised, slender and strong, on the brow of a huge dragon, as it plunged through the billows of a raging sea. Light shone from her to redeem the night. She was the inner citadel of the heart. Bezalia, Lady of the Winds, riding the storm-dragon above the world.

* * *

Lumy easily found the place of silence. During the day she'd felt anger and frustration and disappointment and allowed them to happen. They washed over her like sea waves falling on the pebble beach, and she watched them like someone who lived by the sea and was used to the surf; the feelings passed, just as the waves sank down between the stones, and left her untroubled.

Now she sat in a chair in the hotel room in China. Images drifted past her vision, and she let them pass by.

She saw a sandy beach, on a shore that didn't exist anymore. It was the coastline of her childhood, in a different era of Singapore. The child Lumy, wandering on those shores, found a teeming wealth of tiny life on the mudflats exposed by the ebbing tide. Under her feet with every step, she encountered crabs and small shelly creatures, their little lives jostling and layering over each other. All gone now, those beaches buried under rock and clay, but Lumy did not hold to the memory.

Her vision carried her beyond the shore into the warm shallows. The same profligacy of life was there. Each litre held a million tiny creatures, drifting in the rich nutrient waters. Night fell. Myriad tiny lights hung in the depths. Every creature glowed with the life within it, and lines of light ran between them. Traceries of light threading the darkness. Branching constellations, swaying in the equatorial sea.

Lumy knew that she and Peter and Alex and Katrina were specks of light, in that glowing ocean. They were joined together, part of the vast network of life floating in the limitless sea.

All earth is one, Bezalia said. *All life is one.*

The images were gone from Lumy's mind. The echoes of universal harmony remained, and to these she listened.

Chapter Four

Breakfast at the hotel was more coarse white buns, and a dish of hard-boiled eggs. Old Loo drove up and they put wheelchair and bags into the taxi. He knew where to find the office of Peidong Air. Eventually their tickets were endorsed, and they were told that they had been given seats on the evening flight to Zhengzhou.

'We should go to the airport at once, tell the clerk we are there,' said Lumy.

'Our seats are properly confirmed,' Katrina explained. She was used to being patient with Lumy, who was a generation older, who had never held a job, who didn't know how travel was organized. 'We just have to check-in three hours ahead.'

'Are you sure that they will keep the seats for us?' said Lumy.

Katrina opened her mouth to reply, then stared at Lumy speechlessly.

'You've got a point there,' said Peter. 'I think we have a better chance of getting on the plane if we are at that desk the moment it opens.'

'You know what?' growled Alex. 'I think these people always overbook. This business about endorsing the tickets—maybe it is not true, the bastards just say that to have an excuse to bump us off the plane!'

'We should go as early as possible,' said Lumy, 'and stand at the desk even before it opens.'

'We'll go there right after lunch,' said Alex.

A meal in a good restaurant was something Alex had been promising himself ever since he'd known he was coming to China. He was a hoarder, a collector, of eating experiences. He expected not just pleasure for the eyes and stomach, but an experience that would be significantly different from Chinese meals in Singapore or Hong Kong. And he had managed to convince himself that this meal would be the high point that would console him for all the previous frustrations. He questioned the waiter at some length before ordering.

The food arrived and cheerily Alex urged his friends to eat, and himself ate largely. He mouthed the food judiciously and gave his opinion on each dish.

The steamed fresh-water carp had a muddy flavour. The *baichai* vegetables were overcooked and the oil smelt rancid. The chicken cooked with beans was bony and tough. The noodles were soggy instead of crisp.

'It's okay, it's good enough, Alex!' Katrina said. Alex went on grousing and carping. At the end of the meal, he looked at the bill and burst into a rage. The bill was ridiculously high. He would complain to the local tourist association (he knew there wasn't one). He would write to the papers so that no Singaporean visitors would ever visit this restaurant. Eventually he paid the bill, and they went to the airport again.

Once more, they sat side by side on a wooden bench with Peter's chair in front of them.

'Seems like we've been in this airport for days and days,' said Katrina. 'I will be so glad to get out of it.'

'Well, maybe we've learned something about China,' said Peter.

'I've noticed that they sure don't do things like we do!' Katrina laughed.

'What about the people, what have you noticed?'

'They seem so unhelpful; they don't reach out to strangers. Even among themselves, they're like some of the Chinese-educated Singaporeans, they don't do much touching or eye-contact.'

'They protect their inner space,' Peter agreed. 'They don't have easy intimacy. How about you, Alex? What have you learned?'

'Me?' Alex laughed in surprise, 'these people are so backward, what is there to learn from them?'

Peter grinned. 'Well, you could learn about why you lose your temper!'

Alex blinked. 'Just now in the restaurant,' Lumy said earnestly, 'you got very angry about the bill! Very often, Alex, you get angry, and you grumble and complain!'

'Yeah, I guess I do,' Alex said, looking abashed. 'I like to make sure that I get my money's worth, that I'm not being swindled.'

'It looks as though you enjoy it when you can complain a lot,' said Lumy. 'You would feel like you were missing something, if you had nothing to complain about!'

Alex paused, his mouth open and his breath held, silenced by the truth of Lumy's observation.

'How do you feel when you complain, Alex?' Peter asked gently. 'Do you feel more powerful, in charge of the situation?'

'Yes. I feel stronger,' Alex admitted. 'It seems to make me feel better.'

Katrina, watching this exchange in fascination, suddenly had a question to ask. 'What does Bezalia say about this, Alex?'

Alex paused a moment, eyes focusing inwards. 'Bezalia says, "Why don't you kick this habit,"' he reported gloomily.

Peter smiled. 'Let's do Listening.'

* * *

Alex's watch beeped and they opened their eyes to the bustle of the airport. Someone was watching them closely. From among the crowd of staring onlookers came a man with Chinese features, wearing American casual clothes. He spoke in English, 'Hello! It's good that you meditate in this place!'

He stuck out his hand to shake theirs vigorously. 'I'm Tony Li!' He handed out business cards printed in Chinese and English: Tony Li Tsung-shi, Producer, Hong Kong Eravision. 'You're from Singapore, yes? I could guess, I heard you speaking! What are you guys doing here? Where are you travelling to?' His hands gestured non-stop while he talked, like the hands of deaf people signing. His eyes danced with quick laughter.

'We're trying to get to a place called Chengshen,' Alex said. He felt immediate liking for the Hong Konger. In his mind the local people were an alien for 'them'; Tony Li was part of a familiar world, he was one of 'us'.

'I just came from Lhasa,' said Tony Li. 'Making a film about the Tibetans. My camera men have gone back to Hong Kong already to do the editing. The government doesn't want me filming in Tibet, but how can they stop me? They say Tibet is part of China, so is Hong Kong, so how can they stop me from going in? There is so much interest in America about Tibet, but the Americans can't get in. I went to Los Angeles and there were just too many television companies asking me to help them to make this film. I made it myself!'

He told them that Westinghouse was among his financial backers, and Microsoft was going to distribute the finished film. They did not know whether to be impressed or to think he was talking fantasy. Next, he was telling them he knew the Dalai Lama well, visited Dharamsala regularly to meditate with him, and had made a film about the Dalai Lama's pilgrimage to Lourdes and Fatima.

'So, when I saw you Singaporeans meditating, sitting in a crowded airport in the middle of China and meditating, I said, 'Hey, that's sublime! I must talk to these people!' So, why are you in China? Why are you going to Chengshen?'

'It's to do with the famine of 1959–61,' Peter told him. 'Have you heard of it?'

'The big famine in '61? My mother talked about it. She had relatives in Kwangtung. They were hungry because the whole country suffered from floods and droughts which damaged the harvests.'

'The harvests were not damaged,' Peter said. 'The grain was taken away from the peasants. Thirty million people died of hunger; can you believe it?'

'Yes. Yes. In Tibet they said that the Chinese who conquered them punished their rebellion by seizing all their harvests. In some places, more than half the people starved to death. And you say the same thing happened in China! I wonder whether my mother knows anything about this, I can ask her!' He pulled out a cellular phone.

'Where's your mother?' Alex asked.

'Causeway Bay, she has a very nice apartment near the sea.' Incredulous and amused, they watched Tony Li talk to his mother in Hong Kong.

His mother must have been used to such phone calls. When Li's rapid-fire Cantonese halted, he listened for several minutes, nodding and repeating 'Ah-huh.' He ended the call.

'She says she remembers the famine. In the fall of 1961, the authorities admitted there was hunger, and people were encouraged to send food to relatives in the PRC. My mother says the lines of people at the Post Office, to send away the parcels, stretched along one street and down the next. The PRC put four hundred per cent tax on each parcel. My mother's cousins got the food, and it saved them from dying of hunger.

'My mother thought the famine was in the south provinces only, maybe a few thousands died. She did not know the famine was all over China. I asked her if she knew thirty million people died. And the way she answered, she thought I had said three hundred thousand. Maybe she heard me say thirty million, but she couldn't believe it. I did not tell her that I said thirty million,' Tony Li said, dragging on his cigarette.

Peter told him the story in more detail, showed him printed materials. Tony looked at the photographs and articles with close attention, all his energy converted into intent listening, as though he were recording every word.

He showed no puzzlement, at the purpose of their journey. 'To light candles in the field where many people died, you are saying 'sorry' to the dead. That's sublime! You are making reparation to them. You are trying to mend the karma.'

Tony Li's company brightened and enlivened the last hours that they passed in Dongshandu airport until they were called to board their plane.

They lined up to have their hand baggage checked. An official examined Peter's zipcase and pulled out a book, with Chinese characters above the English title on the cover. 'What is this?' he said. He leafed through it, examined the illustrations. He went into his office, taking the book with him.

'What's that book, Peter?' said Katrina.

'It's the book by Jaspar Becker. *Hungry Ghosts: China's Secret Famine.* Maybe that book is banned in China, they don't want people to talk about it!'

'Oh my god, is he going to stop us from boarding the plane?'

An anxious fifteen minutes passed before the official returned. The book was confiscated, but they were allowed to board their flight to Zhengzhou.

BOOK TWO

Before Dongshandu

Chapter Five

At half-past nine on a Sunday morning, the walkways near Marine Parade market were crowded with people going for breakfast, or on their way to do the weekend shopping. Between the corridors, at an intersection of the covered paths, was a small open plot covered with grass. In the middle of the open space a girl stood at a microphone, singing. Behind her a man in a wheelchair played a keyboard.

The melody was amplified at a low pitch that barely rose above the clatter of the intersection. It was a thing of long notes in echoing minors. The words were repeated over and over again. *Listen. Listen. Someone is calling you. Listen, listen and hear.*

Alex stopped with his family for a moment. Cynthia was hurrying towards the shops and four-year-old Russell was tugging at his hand. Alex stopped and looked at the singer and cocked his ears to catch the thread of sound through the hubbub.

Someone is calling you. Listen, hey listen! Listen, listen and hear.

The girl wore jeans and a tee-shirt bearing the words *All Life is One.* She sang into the microphone in a strong, pure voice, and the man at the keyboard made the melody carry her voice to some lofty, unearthly realm.

Alex stood motionless. He was frowning a little and his jaw hung slightly open. His eyes stared at the girl, a little out of focus behind his Rodenstock eyewear. The song he heard seemed simple and incomprehensible, like a folksong from an alien planet. Its minor keys twisted his guts. The hair on the back of his neck stood up.

Cynthia paused because she noticed that Alex had stopped. She looked where he was looking, saw the girl, heard the song. 'Must be promoting some show,' she said. 'Maybe that new nightclub?' Alex did not reply.

'Nice voice. But no special costume,' Cynthia said.

The song kept climbing through changing keys as though it was going somewhere, and then it started again from the beginning. It seemed to be working towards some answer to a question, but Alex couldn't hear what it was.

'Well, come on. Let's go to the market,' Cynthia urged Alex, in some puzzlement. She took his elbow, gently urging him along. She had finished dealing with the experience and did not know what else there might be for Alex to pull against her hand and stand still, staring at the girl.

'I want—I want to listen,' Alex muttered.

'Come on, Daddy!' Russell clamoured.

Alex felt that something was just out of his reach. He was dying to hear the resolving chord of that music. He desired that solution the way a randy teenager wants the screen goddess, the way a smoker wants a fag on the fourth day of trying to quit.

'Come on Daddy!' Russell's voice was taking on that whining, now-you've-got-to-pay-attention-to-me note that sometimes made Alex wish he'd had the operation done on himself before ever becoming a father.

'Alex, we have to be back for church by eleven . . . '

'I want—' Alex began again. He fell silent, his mouth open. He raised his hands and let them fall again. Different scenarios swept through his head, one way to respond to the demanding voices and another way that led to alternative paths through his future life.

He saw it happening. *'I want to listen,' he said forcefully. He snapped at Cynthia and insisted on remaining for a few minutes more, despite Cynthia's complaints and Russell's whining. He stood and tried to listen to the song. But he'd already lost his temper and couldn't concentrate on what he heard. The whole experience had been spoiled for him.*

He saw it happening. *He gave up on it and went along with Cynthia's tug on his arm, straining his ears to catch the last thread of song as it was swallowed up in the noise of the market crowds. All day he felt angry with her, feeling he had missed something that he would never find again. A residue of resentment and frustration was added to a list he did not know he was keeping, that fuelled a reservoir of rage.*

He could see it happening, whether he fought with her today or another day. He glanced around him with a kind of desperation. *No-win situation. Both ways I lose, Cynthia loses, Russell loses when we have the final fight and she walks out of the house. Oh, why is life such a mess isn't there any way out . . .*

His rolling eyes went once more to the singer and stopped there. It seemed to him that the singer looked straight at him, as he stood on the edge of the crowd, and her eyes gave him a message. Clear as words, he heard: *You don't have to do anything.* He relaxed. He understood what he was being told. He stood still.

'I want ice-cream, Daddy, I want ice-cream!' Russell said.

'Alex! Hurry up, eh!' Cynthia cried. She stared at Alex. He stood as still as something planted and growing in the pathway. Cynthia pulled at his arm, and his arm was heavy: as though he had become a steel statue covered with warm flesh, and it would take blowtorches and hoists to shift him. 'Alex!'

Alex stood listening to the song. He could hear the voices of his wife and son, see their anxious faces. He did not have to do anything. It was all right for them to fuss and carry on, to panic for a while. It did not disturb him.

'Alex! Alex!'

'Daddy? Daddy!' Russell was beginning to cry.

Alex was giving the song his full attention, and he was so happy, it seemed like the first time in his life he had ever been able to attend purely to one thing at a time. The song seemed to swell up inside him, as though it was glad to be welcomed in. The high notes reverberated in the soundbox of his skull, the low notes throbbed in his belly. The words of the song were etched in the wet tissue of his brain. *Calling, calling, listen and hear.*

Time ran slower and slower. The long notes held and held. There was a moment when he seemed to be suspended in magic stillness and calm, and he saw a figure standing in front of him. It was a motherly woman, dressed in a loose black robe.

There was no one else around, they were in a little world of their own. The woman laughed delightedly. She nodded and smiled into Alex's eyes. She held out her arms with a wide embracing gesture that was like something he remembered from long ago.

Come to me, Alex. Hey, come to me!

Yes, he said. *Hello. I'm here. I'm here.*

Alex, my dear! I'm so glad you came!

Alex stepped close up into an embrace of security and reassurance. *I am Bezalia,* the woman told him softly. *The number is three seven seven, three seven seven seven.*

Thank you, Alex thought he said. *Thank you, thank you.*

Bezalia was gone and daylight returned. Alex found that he was standing on the walkway, the crowds around him. Cynthia was staring at him and tugging at his arm, and Russell was whimpering. Over there the song had ended. The keyboard melody was winding down, and the woman in black was nowhere to be seen.

'Hey, what's the matter, squeaky boy?' Alex said. He swung Russell up in his arms and pressed his face into the softness of the child's cheek. He blew out bubbling breath, making Russell giggle and chortle.

'Alex?' Cynthia said.

'All right, come on!' Alex said exuberantly. 'Guess you've got to buy up the whole market before we go back for church!' Alex smiled into Cynthia's eyes. For a very short moment Cynthia stood still, saw her husband smiling into her eyes, and felt her womb contract inside her. The deep emotional flash confused her.

'Okay,' she said uncertainly. 'Okay, let's go.' Fondly carrying his son, Alex happily followed Cynthia into the bustle of the market.

Next morning, Monday, Alex woke up early and examined his memory like a new lottery winner checking his bank account to see whether the money hadn't flown away as suddenly as it appeared. He found the treasure still there; and if it wasn't quite as sparkling and brand new, factory fresh as it had been at first, he refused to notice it.

All through the market, and church, and Sunday lunch with Cynthia's parents, he had been on some kind of high. The moment when the woman in black had looked into his eyes was like a lamp burning in his mind, spilling light everywhere. He was not irritated by Cynthia's mother's usual gossiping. When she indulged Russell in treats that his parents usually vetoed, Alex smiled tolerantly and asked Cynthia to take it easy.

When they got home after lunch, Alex parked Russell in front of the television and took Cynthia into the bedroom and made love to her. They had time for some really good marital sex, and then more time: to sit in the living room, relax, and watch television with Russell for a while, before they left home again for Cynthia's tennis and Russell's Chinese language tuition and to look in on Alex's parents, and then for dinner with Alex's brother Chuan and his wife, Gracie.

They went to their favourite eating-shop in Siglap. 'Better sit inside, the haze level so high today,' Gracie said.

'Bloody Indonesians,' said Chuan. 'They cannot stop people burning up their forests, we get the pollution.' He was extremely sensitive to the smoke particles, and he had red eyes and a sore throat throughout the haze months.

Over *char kuey tiow* and chicken, Alex wanted to share something of his strange experience. But he could not talk about the feelings he had, about the woman who'd looked at him with eyes of love. The words she had said to him didn't hold emotion, and he found a way to talk about them. He said, 'By the way, I dreamed about a number. Three seven seven, three seven seven seven.'

'Go and buy!' Cynthia said.

'What combination?' Chuan said. They discussed eagerly which combination of the seven numbers to buy. Gracie would buy the numbers from the 4-D office near her place of work. They all believed that a dream could predict winning numbers, like the weatherman could predict rain.

On Monday Alex got to his office and found the usual air of urgency and hurry.

'Hock Chong rang first thing in the morning, they want sixteen tonnes of cement tomorrow,' Miss Lee said. 'Lim Seng Teck asked you to send his tiles by today.'

Alex ran a small building supply company. With the construction boom going on, he couldn't keep up with the demand. Sometimes for one delivery he spent a whole morning on the phone, trying to get stocks.

He got on the line talking to Lim and Choo and Boon. It was a pleasant experience, as he talked to Lim, to envisage him as a fine, wonderful guy and have feelings of goodwill and warmth towards him. Ringing off, with the delivery arrangements confirmed and lunch fixed up for Friday, Alex felt that business could be transformed by benevolence and gentleness towards everyone.

The next supplier, Choo, was uncooperative. He said the parts Alex had ordered had not arrived; Alex suspected that Choo had sent them along to a higher bidder. He fenced verbally with the man for a while, being polite but unable to get past the other's screen of lies. Alex rang off, fuming. He called the next man and was very firm with him and got what he needed. Work went on. It was only in the shower in the evening, that Alex realized that his beautiful mood of love and kindness had vanished.

Two days later, Alex felt as though he had just woken up from a dream. He felt supremely normal. He could remember that he had had a strange experience, and that he had been walking around in a kind of daze. I must have been a bit crazy. Maybe I got too much sun that day, he said to himself. What a brainstorm he had had. Strange mood swings. If that had gone on, he might really have needed a doctor. Back to work.

At midday his sister-in-law phoned. 'Hey Alex! We won it! Four thousand and eighty dollars! Won the 4-D, lah, four thousand eighty!'

'We won it?' Alex was confused.

'The number you gave us. Three seven seven seven. Next week, we will buy the other combination, three seven seven three,' his sister-in -law chattered, 'or should we buy the same number again, sometimes it can come out the same number for two weeks, what do you think?'

'No idea,' mumbled Alex. Now Gracie was treating him like some kind of authority on dream numbers. 'Gracie,' he said, 'what do you think that number is supposed to be?'

'Looks like a phone number,' his sister-in-law said immediately. 'I thought that was where you got it. Whose phone number is it?'

'I dreamed it,' Alex said, and could hardly hear himself. He seemed to hear a low clear voice repeating the number. He saw dark eyes smiling at him, a gaze that said he was infinitely precious. A roseate glow of well-being enveloped his mind. He felt terrific. He sank into it with a sensation of falling, of losing his grip on sanity, while part of his mind blew alarm whistles and phoned the hospital for the men in white coats.

Gracie was gone. Alex stared the phone and picked it up again. The handset beeped at him as he pressed the three and the seven in sequence. Beep deep deep beep deep deep deep. Then the slow croaks of the signal for an engaged number.

The seven tones of the phone numbers echoed in his mind. He broke contact and pressed the buttons again and listened to the tones. Beep deep deep . . . *Listen, oh listen and hear.*

He put down the phone. More notes flooded into his mind. A plaintive melody, full of minors. He could remember the tune now, and the words. Once more, Alex was in a state of yearning, of restless desire. But this time, he had no idea what would satisfy that longing or where to start looking for it.

The only link he had was a phone number which led to an engaged tone. Alex pressed those seven digits at different times during the next few days, with no better result. SingTel assured him that the number was in working order and wouldn't tell him who the subscriber was. Four weeks went by, and he couldn't forget.

There was Alex, getting up from bed at three-thirty on a dark rainy night, haunted by a memory of longing, to press buttons on the phone and listen to a seven-note fragment of melody. He huddled on the white leather couch in his nicely decorated living room. Wind whined at the windows of the seventeenth-storey apartment. Rain whipped at the black glass of the window. Alex's bare feet were cold on the terrazzo floor. He got the engaged tone and cut it off and tapped the seven notes again. He realized that there was a kind of happiness in that moment, alone in the dark with the yearning in his heart. The yearning was keeping him company.

One day when he pressed the seven notes on the phone, there was a ringing sound at the other end. He had barely time to register it, when someone answered the phone.

'Good morning.' A standard, pleasant, receptionist's voice. 'Spiritual Arts Centre.'

'Oh. Ah. Oh,' said Alex. 'Arts Centre?'

'Yes, can I help you?' Pause. Alex was *gabra*, totally flustered. 'Do you want to sign up for classes?'

'Yes. Yes, I'd like to sign up.'

'Which class do you want? Classes are at eight p.m., on Mondays and Thursdays.'

'Thursdays,' Alex said promptly. 'Where's your place?'

'It's in Upper East Coast Road. I'll fax you a map, can you give me a fax number?'

Alex gave his fax number and pulled his wits together. 'Ah. excuse me, I'm not quite clear. What kind of art is it?'

'Oh, if you don't know which one you want, you'd better meet the instructor first. I will set up the interview for you on Thursday night.'

'But what is the class, what are you teaching?'

'It is called the art of Listening.'

Chapter Six

Alex figured that the name 'Spiritual Art Centre' was another of those names, like 'Moral Uplifting Home,' which sounded odd in English but made perfect sense in Chinese.

Cynthia dropped him off on the way to taking Russell for Chinese class. Off Upper East Coast Road they found a big two-storied bungalow with cars parked on the lawn. To eyes used to new buildings and HDB estates, it was old and shabby.

'Wow, such properties are worth a lot now,' Cynthia said. 'Wasted, you know, using it for a school. It could be redeveloped for a good condominium.'

Alex walked in through the front veranda and the big arched doorway. He was early for his appointment. A receptionist smiled at him very pleasantly.

'Mr Alex Lee, is it? Maybe you would like to look around our Centre for a while. Please hold on for a moment, I'll get someone to show you around.'

Alex ran his eye over the noticeboards while he was waiting. There were notices and timetables for classes in hapkido, flower-arrangement, and other things he didn't recognize. Reassuringly, there was a regular slot for 'Listening', Instructors Melissa Choong and Peter Fernandez. However weird Listening might be, it was still something that needed chairs, and a classroom, and was run by people who presumably got salary and CPF.

'Hello, I'm Katrina!' a young woman said. Posh accent, management type. The kind of girl that Cynthia said was 'too educated to get married', but pleasant enough as she showed Alex around the Centre.

There was a gym where people in kung-fu gear were courteously throwing each other around. There was a pottery studio where Alex gawked at clay objects, some of which looked like functional bowls and some which . . . didn't. There were walls covered with students' work in calligraphy and Chinese brush-painting.

'Very artistic,' said Alex, trying to get a handle on what was going on here, and wondering whether he would be expected to do calligraphy.

'Spiritual Arts Centre means all the different kinds of art that are good for the human spirit,' the young woman explained. Alex was further puzzled; he knew little about the human spirit and didn't see how flower-arrangement could be good for it.

'You're here for Listening, aren't you?' Katrina said. 'Do you know why you've come?'

'I want to meet Bezalia,' Alex said, and it was the first time he had spoken the strange name aloud to another person. 'Yes, we'd all like to meet her,' Katrina said agreeingly. 'I have not seen her myself—sometimes I just feel that she's there, know what I mean?'

'Don't we meet her in the class?' Alex asked, disappointed.

'Some people say they see her. Like a vision or something. Others never do see her, however well they meditate. But Melissa and Peter will explain all that to you!'

When Alex got into the meeting room, he recognized Peter Fernandez, the man in the wheelchair, and Melissa, the girl singer.

'I saw you at Marine Parade that day!' Melissa said. 'I'm so glad that you found us!'

'What did you experience that day?' asked Peter. 'Did you see or hear anything special?'

'I saw—I saw Bezalia,' Alex said shyly. 'I would like to meet her again!'

'You saw a woman, huh?' Peter asked intently. 'How old did she seem to be? What did she say to you?' Alex fumbled to describe his experience.

'He's one of yours!' Melissa said, exchanging looks with Peter.

'Yes, sure. You'll be in my Listening class, Alex,' Peter said. 'I have to tell you, that people have different experiences when they Listen. They may come to know the one whom you met as Bezalia, by some other name, or under a different appearance. The differences are not important, but to make things less confusing, you will join my group.'

'Will you teach me to see her?' Alex asked.

'No, I won't,' Peter said, with a surprisingly gentle smile. 'I'll teach you to Listen. The rest is up to you—and to Bezalia.'

Alex followed Peter's wheelchair to a room where several people were already sitting in meditation postures. There were men and women, an elderly couple and a frail white-haired man, a teenager in shorts and tee-shirt. Peter introduced Alex to the group and told him what he had to do.

'When the lights go down, Alex, you sit still and you listen,' Peter said. 'First, you listen with your ears: notice what comes to your ears, then go beyond that. Listen with your mind: notice the thoughts that come to your mind, but do not dwell on them, let them slip away, and go beyond. Listen with your heart. Do you understand? Do you need to ask any questions?'

Alex shook his head. On one level he felt mystified and uncomprehending. On another level he felt he understood what he was here to do. When the lights went out, he sat still and began to focus his mind on whatever surrounded him. First, he was very aware of physical itches and tickles, and the heavy breathing of the old gentleman seated behind him. Presently, these dropped away. He heard his own thoughts scurrying around and around: *What am I doing here, what's going on, this is stupid, I must be crazy . . .*

He disregarded them. He remembered how he had listened to a song one Sunday morning and stillness had encompassed him. Remembering, he felt a sense of comfort and love. He heard a voice calling his name: *Welcome, Alex! I am glad you are here.*

His mind could not hold on to silence for long. Soon the tide of ordinary thoughts flooded back, and for the rest of that session he heard nothing more than the ordinary noises of people sitting together in a room.

'How did you find it?' Peter asked Alex after the session, as the other people left the room.

'Good, it was good, I liked it,' Alex stammered. 'But one thing . . . I don't know whether my church can agree with this kind of thing. Spiritual Arts, we are against Spiritualism you know!'

'We are not practicing Spiritualism.'

'When we go into silence like that . . . they say that if you make your mind empty, a bad spirit could come into it. They say there is this danger of evil spirits.'

'Let me tell you another way of doing Listening,' Peter responded. 'You take one word from the Bible, and let it fill your mind. You just keep repeating the Bible word and Listening to it. You might like to try this next time.'

Alex nodded, in some relief. As he prepared to leave the woman, Katrina came up to him and Peter. 'You should ask your wife to come to Listening!' she said.

Alex looked at her in surprise. He didn't remember mentioning his wife to her. 'I don't think Cynthia is interested in this kind of thing.'

'You should try to get her to come!' Katrina persisted.

'I can try,' Alex said doubtfully.

Katrina spoke agitatedly to Peter after Alex left. 'Peter, I felt I just had to tell him he should bring his wife along!'

'Sure, why not, we welcome everyone to come!'

'I tell you Peter, it wasn't my idea! I had this impulse suddenly, that I had to tell him to bring his wife. I felt such a fool—I just met the man, I don't know his wife!'

'You didn't want to follow the impulse, huh?'

'I tried to resist it, Peter. But it just kept pressing me, stronger and stronger. I got so antsy, so *mangchang*, I couldn't do anything else till I spoke to him.'

'It must be important, then,' Peter said thoughtfully. 'We'll see whether she comes.'

* * *

Alex told Cynthia about his evening. 'You just Listen? Then what? What do you hear?' Cynthia asked.

'You don't . . . you don't really hear anything . . . it's still, it's silent,' Alex floundered. 'Why don't you come with me next week?'

'What for?' Cynthia asked, honestly puzzled. 'You can go if you're interested. I don't mind staying home.'

'Come and try it, I'd like you to come!'

Cynthia, after a lot more persuasion, went to one Listening session with Alex. It was not a success. For the first seven minutes Alex was embarrassed to hear her fidgeting and shifting restlessly. Then she was still, and when the lights went up, she rubbed her eyes and confessed that she had fallen asleep. 'I'm sorry . . . my mind was very bored. I just felt very sleepy!'

However, she had been pleased to be introduced to Peter and the Listening group members, including wealthy Mrs Lumiere Chan. So, in future, Alex was able to tell Cynthia about the Centre's activities, and at least she knew the people that he was talking about.

Chapter Seven

A month later, Lumy invited Alex to bring Cynthia and Russell to the buffet lunch spread at a big hotel. Katrina met Lumy as she drove her Mercedes up to the front of the hotel, with Peter in the passenger seat. Knowing that Lumy usually pushed Peter in his chair, she felt obliged to help the older woman. The hotel porters sprang to get Peter into the chair. Katrina pushed it over the rich carpets and into the lift up to the restaurant.

There were two steps down to the floor area of the restaurant and no ramp. Lumy beckoned to a couple of waiters to lift the chair down the steps.

'Damn place is supposed to be wheelchair-accessible,' Peter said with uncharacteristic ire. 'Lumy rang in advance to confirm that!'

They went past the long buffet table with its extravagant spread, a pleasurable assault on the eyes as well as the appetite. Alex and Cynthia and Russell were already waiting at a table that sparkled with glassware and silver.

'Hey, Cynthia, you look good!' Katrina exclaimed. Cynthia had always been plump, *too fat!* in Katrina's mind, and the first thing she noticed was that Cynthia looked thinner.

'Cynthia! You really lost weight!' Lumy said in concern. She saw that Cynthia's skin was dull and slack. Her hair did not shine. 'Is there anything wrong with you?'

'No, doctor says there's nothing wrong!' Cynthia smiled. 'Russell, say hullo to Aunty Lumy, Uncle Peter, Aunty Katrina . . . '

Lumy took Peter round the buffet tables while the others filled their plates. They were all experienced buffet consumers, with personal strategies to maximize returns in terms of epicurean values and carrying capacity. With smiles of satisfaction, they returned to their table and plunged into their meal.

'I have lost four kilos this year,' Cynthia said, over her heaped plate. 'I haven't been dieting or anything, I don't know why!'

'I asked her to see the doctor,' Alex said. 'He couldn't find anything, but he asked her to take some tests, the results are not back yet.'

'Are you taking vitamin supplements?' asked Lumy.

'Yes, I'm taking multivitamins and iron. My brother Ronald asked me to take *lingzhi*, one of those traditional Chinese medical plants, do you think it's good?'

'Sometimes Chinese traditional medicine is better than Western medicine,' Lumy agreed.

'Cynthia, you should come and join us for Listening,' Katrina said.

Cynthia shook her head and laughed. 'Sorry, I really can't do this Listening you know!'

'You have two choices, Cynthia,' Katrina said strongly. 'You can come in for Listening right away. Or you can spend your money, you can go through the whole drill and take a lot of tests, and in the end when the tests can't find anything you can come in anyway.'

The others looked at her in surprise. 'What's this Katrina?' Peter asked.

Katrina shook her head, and now she looked bewildered and upset. 'I don't know why I said that. I couldn't help it! I just had to say it!'

Cynthia was impressed. 'I don't mind coming down to the Centre some evening.'

'Tell you what,' Peter suggested. 'Come after the regular class on Thursday, after the other people go home. A few of us can stay back and try to help you with it.'

* * *

The next week Cynthia came with Alex to the Spiritual Arts Centre, where Peter and Lumy and Katrina were waiting.

'How are you, Cynthia?' asked Lumy. 'Did you get your test results?'

'Tests all negative,' Cynthia said cheerfully. 'But the doctor recommended some food supplement for me to take, we bought six packets, quite expensive. And my Russell, he reminds me to take it every day. He says, "Mummy, drink your special milk!"'

Peter listened to the chatter with a small frown between his eyebrows. A kind of discomfort had seized him as soon as he greeted Cynthia. It was a feeling of emptiness, centred in the middle of his body.

'I'm glad you came tonight, Cynthia,' he said. 'I have a feeling that what's wrong with you is not a physical illness, but something at a spiritual level. And that's something we specialize in!'

The word 'specialist' sounded reassuring to Cynthia. She nodded.

'I know you have difficulty in accessing your inner self,' Peter went on. 'I'm going to suggest that the four of us here will join forces, as it were, to help your mind open up to what is troubling you. Is that all right?'

'Yes, that's fine,' said Cynthia, mystified but trusting.

'Wait,' said Katrina suddenly. She spoke in the strong voice they had heard twice before: as though another spoke through her. 'Be warned. When you open doors, what comes through may trouble you as well.'

Peter looked at Katrina and nodded. He asked, 'Is it dangerous to us?'

'It may distress you, but if your hearts remain constant it cannot harm you,' Katrina heard herself saying.

'Will we be able to help Cynthia?' Peter asked.

'If you decide to do this, you will help to heal the wounded world,' said the voice. 'I will be with you all the way.'

In the silence that followed, they looked wonderingly at each other. 'You heard what she said,' Peter said at last. 'Do you still want to go ahead with it?'

'Yes,' Lumy said at once.

'Yes,' said Alex, not fully understanding what he had heard, but believing that Bezalia thought it was a good idea.

'Yes,' said Katrina, bowled over by the weird experience of hearing those words come out of her mouth.

'All right, let's do it,' Peter said. 'Cynthia, can you come and sit down here, with your back to me?' Cynthia sat on the low stool in front of Peter. 'Alex, you sit in front of her, take her hands in yours. Katrina—next to Alex, your hands on top of his.'

Alex and Katrina took their places, holding Cynthia's hands. Lumy stood next to Peter and put her hands on Cynthia's shoulders. Peter put one hand lightly on Cynthia's head. They all stopped moving.

Silence came down and seized them, a deep stillness beyond their usual experience. Katrina and Alex felt their thoughts halt as though their minds had been struck dumb. It hit Cynthia like an avalanche, and she dropped, not wondering or questioning, into a profound and blissful state of rest.

Lumy saw the vision of the oneness of life. Traceries of light threading the darkness, branching constellations, swaying in the equatorial sea.

As Peter sank into stillness, a sense of apprehension came with him. The uneasiness he had felt was growing, increasing to nausea and revulsion—of what, he did not yet know. Something unpleasant awaited him, and he had a choice. He could resist it, push it away. Or he could listen to it and let it come.

Behind his closed eyes, he seemed to see a featureless white expanse, like clouds or swirling mist. He felt cold. He began to see a stony landscape. The stones were white, veiled in white mist. Here and there lay crumbling things that might have been bones. There was no life, no growing thing.

A feeling of desolation swelled within him, a sickness in his guts and weakness in his limbs. Grief and horror flowed from the landscape he was looking at. A sense of suffering was embedded in everything he saw. It ached through his soul, a despair beyond words.

With hard-achieved surrender, learned over many years, Peter let it enter him and fill his mind. It went on and on. His consciousness reeled and faded. He sank down out of the whiteness into dark. To where it was cool and lightless. There was peace.

Chapter Eight

Lumy stirred and brought the others back from stillness. They opened their eyes and stared in alarm at Peter sitting slumped in his wheelchair, his face wet with sweat and tears.

'What happened Peter?' Lumy asked with concern.

'A lot of bad feelings,' Peter muttered. He put one hand over his eyes. 'I felt—cold. Whiteness. Very desolate, dead. I can't—I don't want to talk about it now!' Lumy nodded. She stood behind Peter's chair and began to knead the tight tendons and muscles of his neck.

'Are you okay Peter?' Alex said anxiously. 'Should we take you to hospital?'

Peter shook his head. The hospital would take one look at the wheelchair, with its story of chronic pain, and write him off as a druggie on a bad trip. All he wanted was to sit quiet and rest.

'What does it mean?' Katrina asked.

'I don't know,' Peter said. Lumy's rings flashed with the movement of her fingers and Peter took a deep breath, lifted his head. 'I'll be all right,' he said. 'Cynthia, are you okay?'

'I'm fine,' said Cynthia. 'It seemed like I just had a deep sleep. I feel very nice now actually, refreshed and relaxed.'

'Relaxed and refreshed, that's good,' Peter said.

'What's going on!' said Katrina crossly. *Stupid,* she scolded herself, *you look like a fool for repeating questions!*

'For now, it is a mystery. Does mystery bother you, Katrina?' Peter smiled at her. 'We'll have to wait, see whether it becomes clear as time goes on—okay with you?'

'But I want to know—now!' said Katrina, crosser than ever. *Now I really look foolish!*

Peter laughed quietly. 'The desire to know comes from your need for security and control, doesn't it? Learn to be comfortable with not knowing, Katrina! Okay, people—let's call it a night.'

* * *

At two a.m. Alex woke suddenly, and found himself lying in bed, cold and drenched in sweat. He thought Cynthia was calling him. He threw off the sheet and sat up. He felt dizzy and weak, his legs shook as he put his feet on the floor and got up, and the floor dissolved beneath his feet. He woke up and found himself in bed, struggling with the sheet.

He got up and thought he walked to the door that melted like wax as he touched it; and he awoke again in bed. He struggled to rise. The nightmare kept looping and he did not know whether he was awake or asleep, feeling sick with paralysis and frustration, with a growing sense of urgency that Cynthia needed him.

'Alex! You have to get up!' a voice said, Katrina's. She was there, pulling his arm. 'Come on! You can't just laze away like that!' With immense relief Alex got up as she pulled at him. He was out of bed and out of the room.

Outside the room they stood on a white plain under a white sky. A road made of granite slabs ran through a stony landscape, patched with white mist. Lumy was on the road too, and so was Peter, hunched in his chair, his arms wrapped round his body. 'Come on,' he said hoarsely. He began to roll his chair, bumping over the uneven road.

Wisps of mist clung to the stones. White tendrils eddied around the wheels of the chair and around their legs. 'What's this sticking to me—' Katrina said. Mist seemed to cling around her. Her outline blurred and wavered. She was no longer walking with them on the road. She had disappeared.

Peter's wheelchair squeaked. Its chromium push-handles were dull and rusty. It stopped rolling. One wheel broke off. The chair collapsed and fell on its side. Peter fell with it and lay motionless on the road.

Lumy looked at Alex. She seemed to speak but he could hear no sound. Silently, she moved away from him, vanishing into the distance.

In front of Alex the stony road ran through the white land. There were low treeless hills, and fields in which no green thing grew. There were piles of rubble that might have been fallen walls. Over all hung a sense of huge anguish, vast as the white sky overhead.

Alex was overwhelmed. He sank to his knees. He could not bear the weight of pain and depression. He covered his head with his arms and grovelled on the road, trying to find escape. He closed his eyes and pressed his face against the hard stones.

He opened his eyes in darkness, choking and sobbing for breath. He was in bed, face pressed into his pillow. Tears were streaming down his cheeks. A great sorrow still filled him and ached in his heart. He lay in bed, unable to move.

He wanted to get up, go to the bathroom, shake off the dream. But he was not entirely awake, he was awake enough to know that, and he was falling asleep again. He struggled against it. He was afraid to sleep again. The dream of the white road and the empty land lay in his mind like a pit waiting to swallow him up. He was frightened, as he felt himself slipping back towards sleep.

He did not dream of the white plain. Instead, he saw a country whose outlines might have been the same, a place of level fields and low hills, under a blue sky with soft clouds drifting through it. The fields were full of water. Green grass and bushes grew around them, on the banks of earth which held the water.

Alex saw a woman's face in the fields. A woman huge as the plain, her thighs the distant hills, her body the land nearby. Her face lay below the water in the fields, and the cloud reflections sailed over it. Shoots of rice grew on her eyelids and her cheeks. She smiled upwards through the water at the sky.

A voice came to him. *All earth is one. All life is one.*

He fell into deep and peaceful sleep, and never remembered this gift of solace.

* * *

Peter phoned Alex the next morning.

'What did you dream about?' he asked.

The dream of the white plain, the empty land, was a cloud of misery hanging in Alex's memory. He was afraid that talking about it would bring back the full force of that misery. He told Peter some of it.

'It was just terrible . . . I don't know how to tell you how terrible it felt.'

'Like being dead, huh? Like being dead and still alive enough to know how awful it is.'

'Yes! Yes, it was as awful as being dead . . . '

'And we were there, the rest of us? And we died?'

'Yes, you and Lumy and Katrina, you all sort of disappeared . . . '

'I know,' Peter said. 'I had the same dream.'

'You . . . dreamed the same dream?'

'A white road, made of ashes, through a burned-out land. You and me and Lumy and Katrina. Wind came and blew the ashes. It blew all three of you away. And me—the bitter wind blew the flesh off my bones, I was just a naked skeleton, and then the bones blew away too and there was nothing left of me at all.'

Alex didn't know what to say to Peter. 'What—what does it mean?'

'My dream means the same as yours. They are both about death and suffering.'

Alex was silent. The words reverberated ominously through his mind.

'I called Lumy and Katrina this morning,' Peter said briskly. 'You know what?'

'Couldn't be—the same dream?'

'Other versions—but the same thing. We'll meet them tonight. We have to talk.'

* * *

They met at a coffee-shop near the Centre. 'So, what does it mean?' Alex demanded. 'Why are we all dreaming? Does it mean that something is going to happen? Such terrible dreams, like we want to die already!'

'Let's take it one step at a time,' Katrina said. Alex saw, incredulously, that she was holding a notepad and pen, ready to take notes on this bizarre stuff. 'First, we should define the common features of this dream we have all shared.'

'I could not see anything,' said Lumy. 'Only I was in the white place, and I was suffering and suffering till I couldn't stand it, and I had to wake myself up.'

Alex gaped at her. 'You mean you can wake yourself up if you want to?'

'Oh yes, if I want to . . . I knew I should try to stay in the dream,' Lumy said regretfully, 'because I knew it was very important. But I just could not take it anymore.'

'I think the common features are cold, and whiteness,' Katrina said.

'The same things I felt, when we meditated with Cynthia,' Peter said. 'Feelings of death, despair, and bitter suffering.'

'But what the hell does it all mean?' Alex repeated. 'Cold and white, is it the North Pole or what!'

'It is some place where a lot of people suffered,' said Lumy. 'They suffered so much, that their feelings are still in the place where they died.'

'What are you talking about!' Katrina asked. *Silly old woman,* said her mind.

'Once I went to Valley Forge in the States,' said Peter. 'It was an old battlefield. I felt so much grief and sorrow hanging over the place, and it wasn't just me, others felt it too. I've heard it is the same at Auschwitz.'

What nonsense! Katrina thought. *I can't believe a smart guy like Peter is so credulous!*

'Katrina, try to believe that there are other forms of perceptions besides those you are used to,' said Peter. 'Many people do pick up such projections, without realizing it. I think that could be what's happening with Cynthia.'

'I think it's in China,' Katrina said suddenly. 'I remember now, there was a building there, its roof had those up-turned corners, like a Chinese temple.'

'I have never been to China!' said Alex. 'Why would I dream of China?'

'Has Cynthia been to China?' Peter asked.

'No, she's never been! What's all this got to do with Cynthia? She's not having any crazy dreams!'

'But she's losing weight. As though she's getting the side-effects.'

'The dreams are so bad,' Lumy said. 'Like you said, Alex: so much bitter pain, it's enough to kill somebody.'

'No!' Alex cried. 'It's got nothing to do with Cynthia!' His voice was very loud. Cynthia was his anchor to the real world that contained his church, his family, everything he knew. The fact that she couldn't meditate only confirmed for him that, while he himself might be drawn into strange paths, her cheerful mundane soul was his lifeline to sanity.

'We are all getting the dreams from some outside source,' said Peter. 'But they started coming after we linked with Cynthia. She is the key.'

Alex jumped to his feet. 'Cynthia's not like that! She doesn't get depressed! She never has such bad, lousy feelings. They are not coming from her. They can't be!' He almost ran out of the room and jumped into his car. They heard his car speeding away through the night-time quiet of Upper East Coast Road.

* * *

Alex drove home fast, gripped by an upsurge of revulsion for Peter and his friends. That night he lay awake for hours. The doctrines of his church, which he had put out of his mind since he began Listening, rose up and accused him of worshipping a false god. He had always been uneasy about who or what Bezalia might be.

On Sunday, he went to his church and sought out an elder whom he trusted. He asked what the Bible had to say about spirits, and he already half-knew what the answers would be.

Elder Lim Boon Seng agreed that spirits should be recognized as good or bad by the results of their action that were seen in people's lives. Alex realized that the awful fear in his dreams, was a sign that Bezalia was an evil spirit. He was full of remorse, at having submitted to her spell.

What about the love you felt from her? asked a small inner voice—not Bezalia's, he was sure he was not listening to her anymore. *Could you be mistaken in that?*

Yes, I could, Alex replied. *I was deceived by Satan's disguise!*

He became horrified at how far he had been led astray. Peter and Melissa were tools of the evil one. Their kind words and friendship were deceptions. He began to feel violently angry with people who were so evil, while they seemed so pleasant and harmless. They should not be allowed to do these things! They should be stopped!

And after a week of brooding Alex decided to take action so that no more people would be harmed and deceived.

Chapter Nine

Peter called Alex to ask him to drop in for a beer. 'No, no, I'm very busy at present!' Alex said hastily and put down the phone. The next Thursday evening, ten minutes before Listening was due to begin, the class was assembled—Melissa, an old man, and a dozen others who met regularly—but Alex was not among them.

'Usually he is so early,' said Lumy. 'I hope he's not dropping out.'

Failure, Katrina labelled Alex in her mind.

'I tell you what it was, he got very upset by those dreams,' Lumy said. 'He got so angry that night.'

'We'll start without him,' said Peter. He rolled his chair to the front of the room. The group settled themselves. 'Listen to stillness,' Peter said. 'Listen to silence.'

There was a knock on the door. Katrina expected to see Alex enter, but it was a complete stranger who pushed the door open and stepped in. A man in a white, long-sleeved shirt and a pair of dark trousers, with an air of held-in power. Behind him, another man with a stronger swagger and menace. 'Who is in charge here?' demanded the intruder.

'I am,' Peter answered, rolling his chair forward.

'Is this a religious group?' said the stranger.

'Yes!' Katrina cried, sensing that this was the right answer. But Peter replied, 'No this is not a religious group. This is the Listening group.' He spoke calmly, trying to convey reassurance to the people in the room.

He could sense their shock and alarm amounting to fear. Many
of them had been brought up to be afraid of the civil authority:
he could remember his own mother threatening him, 'You keep
on doing that and I'll call the policeman to take you away!' On
this irrational substrate was built their awareness that things like
this did happen. Once in seven years or so, an obscure bunch of
people were accused of activities that were harmful to society
and the state. You read in the newspapers that they'd been raided
and arrested and put on trial. Local voices said the trials were fair,
commentators from other countries said that they weren't.

People not following the legal arguments, seeing only the
drama of the big state machine lined up against small individuals,
had the impression that there was a danger, of the arrest and
imprisonment of innocents who had just happened to get out of
line. How strong you thought this danger was, depended on how
much you trusted the world in which you lived.

'We are from Special Branch,' said the stranger. 'We have had
a report that there is an unauthorized gathering engaged in cult
activity.'

'We are not a cult!' Peter said. 'We practice a form of
meditation.'

'Is it some kind of spiritual activity?' said the man.

'Yes. This is a spiritual exercise,' Peter said.

Wrong answer! Katrina's instincts cried again.

'We received a report that you are engaging in occult Satanic
practices,' said the man. The fear level in the room increased.
They knew that Satanic cults had been banned as being harmful
to society. But Peter laughed in real amusement.

'Occult practices! Inspector, I presume you know what a
Satanist outfit looks like? Does this room look like a cult centre?'

The inspector looked round the room. It was very clean and
uncluttered. The only decorations were a basket of flowers, and
framed photographs of the Himalayas on the walls.

'You can look round the whole building,' said Peter. 'Check for hidden worship rooms or whatever. I don't think you'll find anything that looks like Satanic practice.'

The inspector's voice was different when he next spoke. It was as polite as it had been all along, but a lot of the threat had gone out of it. 'Can you tell me what do you do here?'

'We practice Listening. It is a form of meditation.'

The inspector referred to notes. 'Your business is registered as the Spiritual Arts Centre. It is registered for teaching martial arts, flower arrangement, Chinese painting. It does not say Meditation.'

'Our registration says, *and other arts of spiritual development.* That covers meditation.'

'Are you affiliated to any religious organization?'

'No, I told you we are not a religion.'

'The government does not interfere with freedom of religion,' the inspector said. 'But we have found that cults and unauthorized spiritual practices can pose a danger to society.'

'I don't think we fall into that category,' Peter said with a smile. 'Take a look at the place, Melissa will show you around.' Melissa left with the two inspectors. The group remaining in the room hummed with agitated conversation and speculation.

'Look, relax folks,' said Peter. 'This is nothing. It is not a problem. Someone made a report on us, for whatever reason, so the authorities have to follow up the report and investigate. But there's really no problem.'

'We can continue to do our Listening now,' Lumy said.

Peter smiled and shook his head. He thought not many people besides Lumy would be able to put aside their worries, to concentrate on silence.

The inspectors came back. 'Thank you for your cooperation,' the lead investigator said to Peter. 'You understand. Someone makes a report, we have to follow up on it,' he added, almost apologetically.

'So, are you satisfied, that we're not running any cult here?'
Peter asked politely.

'I will send in my report, it's okay. You get yourself properly
registered as a meditation group.'

Peter paused. 'In the meantime, we will carry on with our
meditation class.'

'When you have registered yourselves, you can resume your
activities.' The inspector explained the situation to Peter in a
friendly way. 'At present you are not registered for this activity.
Your group here is considered as an unlawful assembly. So, you
go and register yourselves then you can carry on.'

'Do you mean,' Peter said carefully, 'that we cannot have our
meditation session tonight?'

'You are not registered for meditation,' said the officer. A
hardening of his stance implied that he was there to see that all
regulations were heeded.

Peter turned to the group. 'Okay, people. We won't have
Listening here tonight. You can go back and do it at home,' he
said serenely.

There were protests and worried questions. 'Look,' Peter said.
'You guys are already supposed to be Listening twice a day on
your own. It's no big deal if we don't get together for a while. How
long? I have no idea how long it will take to do the registration.'

Katrina, struggling with her own consternation and dismay,
saw with amazement that Peter was smiling light-heartedly:
'Maybe if you can't come here for Listening every week, some of
you will be encouraged to practice more regularly at home!'

* * *

Katrina waited impatiently for the rest of the group, who didn't
know Alex well, to disperse. 'It's Alex! It's Alex!' She could hardly
contain her rage. 'I'm sure he's the one that made a report on us!

Saying that we're a satanic cult, that's just like him! He was always afraid that Bezalia was some kind of devil or something.'

'Yes. He's afraid,' Lumy said.

'I have a cousin in the Police,' said Peter. 'I will ask him if he can find out who filed the report on us.'

'I'm sure it's Alex!'

'Probably,' Peter agreed gravely.

Katrina could not understand how Lumy and Peter were reacting. They seemed more disappointed than angry with Alex. 'What a bastard, this Alex! We were so good to that guy! We were trying to help his wife, we spent time with him,' Katrina remembered the hours of convivial friendship. 'How could he do this to us! Bloody bastard!'

'He was very upset about the dreams,' Lumy said.

'I'll get Melissa to do the registration tomorrow,' Peter said. 'It shouldn't take long to get approval, then we'll resume the usual classes. But for the present—I'd like to ask you two,' he looked at Lumy and Katrina, 'to do Listening with me. Just the three of us.'

'Yes,' Lumy said, nodding vigorously. 'Yes, we should do that.'

'Why?' Katrina asked, bewildered again. 'I mean I would be happy to do listening with you regularly, but why just the three of us, is there some special reason?'

'Because we are the ones who linked to Alex,' Lumy explained in her slow way. 'We are the ones who can help him now.'

'Help him!' Katrina spluttered. 'Why would we want to help that bastard! He just stabbed us in the back! Hope the bugger goes to hell! No way I want to help him!'

'We have to help Cynthia,' Lumy said.

Katrina hesitated. She wasn't yet ready to say that Cynthia should also go to hell. 'Anyway, what do you mean, help him? You are asking me to do Listening, right? Not to do anything, go out and talk to Alex or anything like that?'

'Right. I am only asking you to Listen,' Peter said, with the glimmer of a smile. 'The four of us are linked, as Lumy says. When one of us has gone away, the other three can keep an opening for him. And for Cynthia too. Don't worry too much about all that, Katrina! All I am asking you to do, is to sit down and do Listening with us—and to know that Alex, who is absent, is still here with us.'

Katrina was silent. Listening was fine, she thought. She didn't understand, didn't believe, half of what Peter was spouting, but she could spend half an hour Listening with him, and nothing to do with bloody Alex.

'Anyway, Peter—I am sure Bezalia is not a devil, but who is she really? Who is Bezalia?'

'Ask her yourself, one day,' said Peter. 'But I think you're too rational, Katrina! I don't know how to give you any answer your mind can accept.'

Lumy set a timer, Peter said the opening words. Katrina began to listen: and all she could hear was the incessant roar of her own anger. Outrage and protest at what Alex had done to them, his betrayal of friendship, his treachery. They went bitterly round and round in her for half an hour. When she got up, she felt exhausted and ill-tempered.

'Thank you for joining us, Katrina,' Peter said. 'Can you come again tomorrow evening?'

'I can pick you up from your office,' Lumy offered.

'No, I—I don't think so,' said Katrina. She was thinking that she didn't want to attempt Listening again for a few days, till she had cooled down a bit. 'I'm quite busy now! I don't think I can come.'

Chapter Ten

'I think I will go and visit Alex,' Lumy said. 'When I tried to phone him, he just hung up the phone on me. I wanted to ask him why he did such a thing, he was so friendly and then he turns against us like that. He didn't want to talk to me on the phone. But we have got to ask him what is happening. Cannot leave it like that.'

Peter looked at Lumy: elderly, beringed, cosmeticized. He thought not many people would have the courage to call someone who hurt them. Or go on afterwards to visit that person.

'Yes, I'm worried about him too,' he said. 'My cousin confirmed, it was Alex who made the police report. I think he did it because he was so afraid of the dreams.'

'He is simply hitting out at us,' Lumy nodded. 'Because he is so frightened. Peter! How are you feeling lately?'

'I've been feeling lousy all day. Not my back . . . Just a sort of general depression . . . '

'Me too, Peter. I am feeling very depressed and irritated and fed-up. But nothing happened, there is no reason why I should be like that—I think I am getting these feelings from outside.'

'My god, yes,' said Peter. 'You're right, Lumy! All this frustration and despair—it's not my own stuff! We've picked up this load of bad vibes, they give us horrible dreams, and make us feel lousy. We get all upset and churned up, and Alex goes storming off in a rage—'

'I'll go and see him.'

'He's probably still upset, he may yell at you some more,' Peter said. 'Do you want to take Melissa with you?'

'No, I think I won't take anyone, I think I go by myself,' Lumy said. She explained with many repetitions that Alex was feeling defensive, and one person would be less threatening to him; for the same reason she would not invade his home but would go to his office.

So Lumy's green Mercedes pulled up in a street near Jalan Besar which was lined with businesses related to the construction industry. She walked into the open shop whose front area was stacked with hardware and found Alex sitting in a glassed-in, air-conditioned cubicle at the back. She knocked on the glass door and pushed it open a crack. 'Hullo, Alex—how are you?' she said cheerily.

Alex stared in disbelief as he saw Lumy picking her way through the front part of his shop. After what he had done to the Listening group, he had not expected to ever speak to any of them again. They must hate his guts now, but he did not expect any of them to come and yell at him—least of all the beaming, wealthy woman he was seeing

He didn't know how to respond to Lumy's greeting. Part of him warmed to her open friendliness, and part of him said that she was the dupe of the Evil One. Mostly he felt defensive, ready to explode angrily as soon as she started to attack him.

'How are you, Alex? How's Cynthia?'

'Fine. Cynthia's fine.'

'Are you sure, Alex? Has she stopped losing weight?'

'She's okay, she's okay!'

'You must look after her, Alex. Take care of Cynthia.' Lumy smiled kindly at Alex. He was wondering when she would start tactfully leading up to the nasty subject that lay between them. As soon as she did, he would change the subject.

Lumy looked straight at him and said quietly, 'You reported us to the police for running a cult.'

Alex stared back speechlessly.

'These two inspectors came in when we just started Listening,' Lumy related. 'They were looking for Satanic worship! They searched the whole house. They did not find anything. They said we have to stop Listening until we get registered with the Registrar of Societies. Alex, can I ask you,' Lumy said, her inexpressive voice almost gentle, 'why did you report us? Why did you say that we are a cult?'

'You are a cult,' Alex said. He was surprised that it was possible to say such a nasty thing to somebody's face without animosity. This whole conversation was weird. 'You worship Bezalia. Bezalia is an evil spirit.'

'We don't worship Bezalia.'

'You let her possess your hearts,' Alex said. Lumy looked at him in silence, and in silence Alex remembered the joy and comfort he had received from Bezalia, the assurance of being deeply loved.

'Did you do this because you are afraid of the dreams?' Lumy asked.

'The evil spirit sent those dreams to me,' Alex said. 'I am under demonic oppression.'

'I don't think Bezalia sent those dreams. They come from somewhere else.'

'I am going to ask the Church elders to pray over me!' Alex said defiantly. 'I will renounce the evil spirit and pray to be delivered from this bondage!'

'Yes, you should do that, Alex!' To his surprise, Lumy agreed enthusiastically. 'You should bring Cynthia also. Both of you should have prayers, to be free from whatever bad influence is on you. You should bring Cynthia to the elders also.'

'I will, then,' said Alex. 'Uh—can I get you a cup of coffee?'

'No thanks,' Lumy said, 'I'm just going. Give my love to Cynthia, huh!'

Alex found himself walking Lumy out to her car just as though she were a good old friend. He watched her drive off, feeling very confused. He couldn't figure out whether Lumy was a servant of Satan. He knew that he himself had done right, in rejecting the works of the devil, and couldn't understand why he felt guilty about it.

Three days later, Peter called Alex on the phone, and Alex only winced a little when he heard the familiar voice. 'Oh, ah, hullo, Peter! Ah, how are you, how are you?'

'How's Cynthia getting on, Alex?' Peter managed to convey enormous concern in those few words and Alex found himself responding to his sympathy in the old way.

'She is still losing weight, Peter! She lost one kilo since last week.'

'Oh dear. I'm sorry about that. And yourself, Alex, how have you been? Had any more dreams?'

'Yes. Yes. Terrible bad dreams, I don't know what! Last Sunday, the church elders prayed over me and Cynthia. They bound the evil spirits and freed us from oppression. I don't know why this is still happening, Peter!' Peter did not reply. 'Peter? Eh—Peter?'

'Alex, I think you should come back to Listening. Is there a problem, with you thinking we are a cult organization?'

'Oh.' Alex had forgotten about the cult concept. His conviction that they were all devils, had somehow melted away. He said weakly, 'The police told me that their inspector found nothing wrong at the Spiritual Arts Centre. I guess I made a big mistake.'

'Let's meet up!' said Peter warmly. 'We aren't allowed to have our usual group sessions yet. It will be just you, me, Lumy and Katrina.'

* * *

Somehow that meeting did not happen for a while. Katrina said she was not free, and Lumy meant to come but her car broke down. Instead, Alex picked Peter up and the two of them went to a pub on River Valley Road. Surrounded by low light and soft jazz music, Peter listened to Alex's worries and talked to him about his religion. Alex was surprised that Peter knew the Bible pretty well and could make a possible case that Listening and Bezalia were in line with Scripture teaching.

But it was Peter's good-humoured and generous approach that went furthest to persuading Alex, that it was all right to entertain this broader view of his faith; that coaxed him away from the panicky fear, of allowing his ideas to change.

Another evening, Katrina was not available, and Peter had to stay home with a bout of back pain. 'Bring Cynthia and Russell to my place for dinner!' Lumy invited Alex, 'I will tell my maid to boil my special chicken soup, very good for Cynthia.'

It was the grandest private home Cynthia had ever visited. She was pleased to sit at the table with Lumy's husband, the boss of Chan Leong Holdings. After dinner Chan Leong watched the news of the Asian financial crisis on television while Lumy brought them to a separate room, soundproofed and airconditioned, with a thick carpet and lots of cushions.

'I can't meditate!' Cynthia repeated.

'Never mind, maybe you can just sit quietly while Alex and I do Listening. When you have had enough you can go to the other room and watch television. Russell, your Mummy and Daddy are going to meditate for a while. Can you sit down on this cushion, and be very very quiet?' To Alex's astonishment, Russell folded his hands and closed his eyes and remained still at Cynthia's side.

Lumy dimmed the lights. Alex began to say his Bible word. He felt at once, the presence in his mind.

I am glad you're back, Alex. You thought I was an evil spirit, did you? Are you okay now?

I'm sorry, Bezalia. I'm so sorry.

You were seeing demons everywhere, weren't you!

I'm sorry! You are not a demon, Bezalia!

No, I'm not, Alex. Know that I love you, and in love, be free of fear.

Who are you Bezalia? Alex murmured, as Katrina had asked before him. And to Alex, Bezalia gave an answer.

I am a wave of the infinite ocean. I am a finger of God.

When Alex came back to ordinary consciousness, Cynthia was still sitting in a corner of the room, watching him peacefully, with Russell asleep on her lap.

'I'm so glad you feel better now!' Lumy congratulated Alex, as though he had just recovered from a serious illness. 'Now we must get Katrina to come and Listen with us.' But that did not happen for a long time.

* * *

No dreams tonight, Peter said, when he had been helped to bed one evening. *No more dreams please, Bezalia.*

I'm sorry, Peter, but I can't divert them. When you four made a link with Cynthia, you started something which must develop over time.

Meanwhile these dreams are driving me bananas! What's holding us up? What are we waiting for!

As always, Peter, what holds you back is pride and ego; it's human woundedness. You are waiting for healing to happen.

Chapter Eleven

Katrina began to feel that as much as Alex the offender had disturbed her peace of mind. Alex, repentant, was even worse.

Lumy rang her up and told her that Alex would be joining them that evening at the Centre.

'What is he coming for?' said Katrina. 'I don't want to meet him!'

'Don't worry, he won't give us any trouble,' Lumy reassured. 'He wants to take us all for dinner after Listening.'

'Won't give us any trouble! He made a police report on us, got us closed down! Now he wants to come back! I don't want to eat his dinner!'

'No, no, Katrina, I think Alex is all right now, he is regretting what he did.' Lumy explained that Alex had had more bad dreams and wanted to talk about them.

'Hell's bells!' said Katrina. 'He does this to us, then he has the cheek to ask for our help! I'm not coming tonight. I don't want to see Alex's face. Excuse me now please, Lumy, I have to get back to work.' She put down the phone and fumed.

Outrage and protest at what Alex had done to them, his betrayal of friendship, his treachery. To let go of these feelings was like making light of what he had done, as though the hurt didn't matter. It was not right for her to give this up: it was as though she agreed it was all right for him to hurt her. She couldn't do that.

Later that day Peter called to ask her to come to Listening. 'I'm not coming. I don't want to meet Alex,' said Katrina. 'After what he did to us!'

'I think he is sorry for what he did,' said Peter.

'So now Alex feels so sorry!' Katrina cried. 'Is it just so easy, say "sorry" and make everything the same as it was before! Hey, sorry no cure!' she growled and hung up.

Sorry no cure. School-playground idiom, taking her back to when Adelina, the leader of the girls' gang, punched Katrina's arm for allegedly tattling to the teacher, and rejected her attempts at apology. 'Sorry no cure!' cried Adelina unforgivingly.

Katrina was excluded from the gang of the girls who were considered smart and successful, for innocently telling the teacher about Adelina's new music tape that she had brought to school. Adelina arbitrarily designated this as telling tales. Katrina was rejected from the gang, labelled as one who failed to measure up, an inferior form of life.

Sitting in her office, Katrina remembered the shame and humiliation of those days. And then another image came to her mind. She saw herself, a well-dressed, capable, decisive executive, sitting in her office feeling crushed because of what some pimple-faced schoolgirl in a blue uniform said to her seventeen years ago! She burst out laughing.

I always wondered how I'd done such a bad thing, she thought. And then, *Maybe it wasn't what I did. Maybe Adelina was just showing her muscle, that the rules were whatever she said they were!*

Katrina smiled and went on with her work. Deep down she felt relieved and blessed, as an old injury was healed.

* * *

'We need to talk about these dreams,' Peter said to Katrina on the phone one evening. 'Have you had them too?'

'What dreams?' Katrina said, not fast enough.

'You have, huh? All of us have been dreaming about people who seem to be starving. We see more detail, than the first dream. Lumy says, it looks like China.'

'Yes,' Katrina said. 'It's definitely China. I saw a picture of Chairman Mao.'

'A picture of Mao?' Peter repeated in amazement. 'Then this is something happening now, in our times! Did any people starve to death in China, during Mao's time?'

'I never heard of any.'

'I thought this happened long ago, centuries ago! It's recent, within our own lifetimes, that's why it packs so much punch.'

'Hey, it's only a dream, Peter!' Katrina said uneasily, 'don't take it as though it was very factual!'

'Katrina, whether you believe it or not, you have the gift of psychic intuition. You get to know things, in a non-rational way. I do take your dreams and insights seriously. I'll ask a historian I know, about recent famines in China.'

'Peter, I don't think I'm irrational!'

'I didn't say you were. Don't be scared of the gift you have. Katrina, we have to talk about these dreams!'

'Sure, you can phone me any time!'

'We need to meet with Lumy and Alex.'

'I don't want to meet Alex,' Katrina said. 'I don't want to see his face.' She refused to be persuaded, even though she knew that her intransigence was an ugly thing—almost as ugly as what Alex had done.

* * *

Katrina didn't like what Peter had said about her intuition. *So strange, so abnormal!* By the time she went to work next day—*no time to do Listening this morning*—she had rescued and rebuilt her mental image of herself: Katrina Leong, Financial Controller, competent and efficient.

She worked through the lunch hour, as she often did. She used the extra time to do a double check on her morning's work, and to read through letters waiting for her signature.

On one letter, the client's name had been wrongly spelt. Katrina called Penny into her office and explained that the correct spelling of the client's name was important to show that the company recognized and valued that customer. Mistakes decreased customer confidence, Katrina carefully explained to Penny, and might have suggested that the company did not give attention to details. Katrina asked Penny to reprint the letter.

Later that afternoon Katrina, passing one of the cubicles, heard Penny talking to another typist. 'So, she caught one mistake in my letter, make her so happy lah! So she can scold me for ten minutes, make her day lah!'

'So, the more mistakes you make, she the more happier lah!'

'She just loves to scold people every day. I feel like changing for another job, boss not so *ngiow.*'

Katrina crept away as quietly as she could. Her heart was pounding in distress. Why did Penny see her as someone meanspirited, who loved to find fault with others? At the moment of discovering the mistake, Katrina recalled, she felt no joy. She felt an unpleasant inner twinge, which was far from delight. *A mistake, over my signature. It becomes my mistake.* Fear.

Katrina was a lawyer's daughter, who'd gone to one of the best schools in Singapore. As long as she could remember, she'd known that society was divided into the best and the rest of the world. She went through her life as a prickly, defensive person, always needing to prove that she was brighter and smarter and more capable than anyone else around. She punished herself mercilessly for every failure. Being ruthless to herself kept her feeling safe.

Once when she was twelve years old, being taken to the museum, she saw a group of children going around with their teacher. One boy had thick lips and nose, his forehead bulged, his eyes were slits. Another girl walked limpingly, dragging a foot, her shoulder hunched and her head twisted to one side.

Katrina's stomach closed up and her throat tightened. She stared at the strange children in revulsion and curiosity. She had always disliked seeing people who were ill, she had a distaste for any kind of deformity.

'Who are they?' she whispered to her mother.

'I think they come from the special school,' her mother whispered back, 'the School for the Educationally Sub-normal.'

The teacher with the defective ones laughed and talked affectionately to them. Another boy walked with leg-braces in a clumsy hobble. Another boy had white skin and white hair and pale eyelashes, and he laughed too loudly in the museum. Lurching along the passage, he passed close to Katrina, and she flinched away. The teacher noticed and gave Katrina an encouraging smile. But Katrina was afraid.

The ESN children were the image of what she feared she might be, less than perfect, defective, only fit to be rejected and despised. She was afraid to be like them.

Chapter Twelve

'Why do you keep on with Listening?' asked Cherry, Katrina's sister. She was ironing her blouse in the living-room one morning, as Katrina uncurled from her posture on the sofa.

It was Cherry who first dragged Katrina to the Listening class in Upper East Coast Road. Cherry, younger, quicker to catch on to passing fads, had heard about it from an office colleague, 'Very relaxing! You just sit still for half an hour, it relieves your stress, lowers your blood pressure!'

'New Age nonsense,' Katrina had said, but 'Come on, how can it hurt you to just try?' Cherry had replied. They went one Thursday evening. Afterwards Cherry said firmly that she didn't see any point in it and refused to go again. Katrina, scolding Cherry for making a snap decision, kept on going, and a year later was still attending and practicing regularly at home. She could hardly have said why. Nothing special happened during the hours of practice. She had never seen Bezalia. But even when she was mad with Alex, even when she had not met with the group for weeks and felt she did not want to talk to Peter and Lumy, she kept on with her daily practice.

'I guess—I go because of Bezalia,' she replied to Cherry. 'You know they say—sometimes she comes and sits with us. I sort of feel she is there.'

'You really love her, don't you!' Cherry said, shaking out the ironed blouse to cool it.

Katrina shrugged. 'Love?' she said dismissively, in the shorthand of sisters: referring to Katrina's two failed relationships, and to Cherry's current status of being joyously engaged to Francis Lim. 'What has love got to do with Listening?'

'You talk about Listening like a kid talks about her favourite teacher! Like you've got a crush on Bezalia!'

'Ha ha, very funny! Do you see me bringing presents for her and writing her little notes?'

'I see you doing your Listening every day like homework. And not going to Sheryl's birthday party to go to the Listening class instead. You didn't give that kind of devotion to your wonderful Joe Tan, except right at the beginning.'

'How can you make that kind of comparison!' Katrina said indignantly. 'You don't know what Listening is at all.'

'I think you love Bezalia,' Cherry said, reaching for her shoes from the shoe-rack. 'Oh Lord, I have to run!' At the door of the apartment, standing on one foot and the other to tug on her shoes, she added: 'Look, try it the other way around—does Bezalia love you?'

The question went right down into Katrina's heart. It seeded and swelled there, like a mine exploding, like a rocket bursting in a chrysanthemum of sparks to fill the sky with light, and the light was the certainty that Bezalia loved her. She sat listening to Cherry's departing footsteps, and this knowledge immersed her and held her still.

Down the corridor, Cherry's voice greeted a neighbour, the man's voice replied. A door banged softly, the corridor was quiet. Katrina sat motionless, enraptured in mind and body, feeling as though there was no point in ever moving hand or foot again.

Like a spectator totally gripped by the last match of the season, like a reader lost in the other world of a gripping romance, Katrina forgot where she was and who she was and even that she was, that she existed. There was no Katrina, only the flow of love. Everything in her was bathed in the inward flood of joy. Without sight, without image, she felt Bezalia close to her and was enfolded in her love as an infant is enfolded in its mother's womb.

Yet her eyes stayed open, unseeingly seeing the room; and in some part of her she knew when it was time to get up, get dressed, go to office.

I don't want to leave, she said to Bezalia in her mind.

I will come with you, Bezalia replied.

Katrina walked to the train slowly, with the feeling and flavour of that experience permeating her, changing her view of the world.

Like eating raw garlic, Bezalia said laughing, *the flavour stays with you all day!*

Will you stay with me? You won't go away?

I will always be with you.

* * *

It was an easy day at the office. There were no meetings; Katrina, in a burst of energy, finished off all her e-mails and made a start on the report she had been putting off doing. At lunch time she avoided going out with Janet and Siok Choon and walked out by herself into Shenton Way. Without planning where to go, she turned away from the towers of the business district and walked briskly along Cantonment Road. She went past a football field and HBD apartments; walking through patches of strong sunshine, and of the thin shade of flame trees with red flowers in their boughs.

In front of her an elderly woman came out of the apartments, holding a little boy by the hand. The woman wore the old-fashioned *samfoo,* and the little boy wore blue pants and a crisply starched, white shirt. Katrina walked slowly behind them. The little boy trotted lightly beside the woman's measured, heavier tread. The small white hand was clasped in the dark wrinkled one. They walked down the path in front of Katrina and stopped at the traffic lights to cross the road.

Katrina didn't know why she was full of liking and affection for the pair. At the traffic light she spoke to them, which was not her custom to do with strangers. She smiled at the old woman. 'Your grandchild?' she asked in dialect.

The woman smiled back: a weather-worn face marked with mild endurance, breaking out in warmth. 'My grandson,' she agreed. Her eyes were almond shaped openings under a broad forehead. Brown pupils set in creamy sclera, almost unscreened by eyelashes, looked at Katrina with kindly interest.

'Are you going to school?' Katrina asked the child. He nodded shyly, and at his grandmother's prompting he piped up clearly, 'St Thomas afternoon school.'

The green man flashed for the pedestrian crossing, the woman clasped the child's hand again and prepared to cross. *Banban jo,* she gave Katrina a friendly farewell. Again, the radiant smile from the wrinkled brown face. The child grinned with a flash of little white teeth.

They crossed the road. Katrina followed them; and in her mind, as in the trance of the morning, were no thoughts, no ideas, nothing but the vision of the smiling old woman and the little boy.

She turned right and came to a sunken courtyard between two blocks of old houses. There were benches in the shade of trees; and an old banyan tree with its interclasped stems and long hanging aerial roots. At the foot of the tree was a flash of red: a few incense sticks in a jar, a rudimentary altar to the spirits of the place.

Katrina sat down under the banyan tree and let the image in her mind take over her being. She saw again a warm friendly smile: a grandmother and her grandson, bound to each other in pure love, love that radiated to anyone who came near.

Above Katrina, the big banyan lifted its branches to the sky, sent its roots deep into the ground. She sensed its joyful life between earth and heaven, its love relationship with baking sun and monsoon storms. In some unfamiliar way of messaging, it gave her teachings of endurance and strength.

What's happening? Am I really communicating with a tree? What is this?

All life is one, said Bezalia's voice. *All love is one.*
Sitting quietly on the bench, Katrina had a sense of divinity dwelling in each material thing. The ancient presence of the tree, and the smile of the grandmother, and Bezalia's awareness within her, flowed through her. Each thing she looked at, the old tree, the stones, the park benches, seemed to be surrounded with radiance. The courtyard was filled with clear light. God was everywhere.

As she rose to look for a cab to go back to office, she knew she had been changed. She would never look in the same way as before, at a tree or an old woman; they would henceforth always be illuminated for her by a new way of seeing, an inner eye of love.

* * *

She walked into office five minutes late, and her colleague Janet met her with a sheaf of papers in her hand. 'Where were you Katrina? Khoon Huat was looking for you. Seems there is a problem with this report.'

'What problem?' Katrina asked, with a sinking feeling. Her boss Khoon Huat had little patience with people who didn't deliver the performance he expected.

'This figure, Katrina. Khoon Huat asked you to check whether it is correct. He said he'll see you when he gets back from his meeting.'

Katrina looked at the figure Janet pointed to. 'What's wrong with it? I checked it . . . ' Then she saw the mistake. She had used the wrong rate of interest, used the rate that had been changed just before the period under consideration. She had forgotten to adjust for the change.

She stopped breathing. She felt numb with shock. *Careless! Incompetent!* Her mind screamed at her. She could not feel the contact of her feet on the floor, as she moved into her own office and sat at her desk.

Her mind scurried around looking for some way to conceal the mistake. Blame the data source, blame the typist, hide the page of the report, burn the whole file and say a stray cigarette destroyed it.

My mistake. My failure. The boss would see her soon. She could imagine his cutting remarks, imagine her own shame and humiliation. A hollow feeling in her gut, a dry mouth and a cold sensation in her face and hands. Her heart pounding and her head feeling faint and far away.

And then, Bezalia was with her, and she felt as though Bezalia's arms went around her.

I made a mistake, Bezalia, I made a mistake!

Yes, you made a mistake. But you're all right, you're okay.

I can't be okay! I made a mistake! I'm destroyed, I'm dead!

Hush. Be still, Katrina, I am here with you.

Katrina's breathing deepened, her body was quiet. She sat at her desk, eyes open and unseeing. In her mind she was with Bezalia, in a sunken courtyard in the shade of an ancient tree.

She was walking through the courtyard. On the sun-baked concrete a child sat playing, a small girl about three years old. The child looked up and smiled. Her mouth was slack and stupid, her face was smeared with dirt and mucus from her nose, her legs wore corrective braces.

The child was Katrina's younger self. Katrina recognized the face of her own self-loathing and mistrust. She shuddered, feeling her heart shrink like she was going to die.

This is me. This is what I am. Not fit to live, not fit to exist in society. She stared at the child, wanting to banish her from sight, wishing her out of existence.

The small Katrina whimpered and made clumsy movements with her arms. She was pitiable and disgusting. *If you don't love me, who will love me?* she seemed to say. Katrina felt paralysed by horror and revulsion.

Bezalia stepped forward. She was there, a woman strong and slender, stooping down to the defective child and holding her close. The child's crying stopped. She wriggled in Bezalia's arms, raised her hand to pat Bezalia's cheek. Bezalia kissed the dirty little face. She looked up at Katrina.

Bezalia's eyes compelled Katrina. She knelt on the hot concrete, close to the child but not touching her. Katrina felt an impulse of pity go through her. She opened her arms, awkwardly embracing the child.

The damp little body pressed against her. The unfocused eyes met hers and the child beamed at Katrina. She chuckled happily and reached up to put her arms around Katrina's neck. Suddenly Katrina felt full of love. She did not care about the dirt on the little hands, the faint sour smell of her hair. She hugged the child tightly.

Bezalia stroked the child's hair. Katrina felt the gentle caress on her own head. Now she had become the child, nestling against Bezalia's breast. The adult Katrina, the one full of masks and defences, was gone. She knew that she was impaired, imperfect, and it did not matter at all. She need never be afraid again.

* * *

Katrina rose from deep trance and found herself sitting at her desk with the report in front of her. She felt well-rested, as though she had been on a week's vacation. She felt great relief, at freedom from fear. It didn't matter what the boss said about her carelessness. It might be unpleasant, but it couldn't wound her. She would not be destroyed.

No need to deny her own fallibility, to strive fearfully for perfection. She had made a mistake and she could forgive herself. 'I'm all right. I'm okay,' she said aloud, and went to meet Khoon Huat.

Chapter Thirteen

On the second of October, Alex met Peter, Lumy and Katrina for Listening. It was the first time he had been together with this group since he had walked out on them.

He stepped into the usual Listening room and saw that no one had used it for a while, the air smelt musty with disuse. He realized again the enormity of what he had done. He had struck a blow at the group that had given him so much friendship and reassurance. His face flushed hotly in an uprush of guilt and shame.

'I—I want to say something first,' he stammered. 'I regret what I have done.' It was hardest of all to say this in front of Katrina. Peter and Lumy were looking at him with kind eyes but he knew that Katrina had been angry, that until this day she had refused to come to Listening if he would be there. 'I was wrong to make a police report on you.'

'You told me, you really believed we were running a cult,' Peter said mildly.

'Yes, I believed it, but I was wrong . . . '

'You made a genuine mistake,' Peter said, and Lumy nodded vigorously.

Alex felt worse than ever. He had hit out against people who were his friends. He saw Katrina looking at him, unsmiling. He spoke to her: 'I reported on the group. I reported on my friends! I am very sorry about it.' He found himself choking on a lump in his throat. 'I am very sorry!'

Katrina's hands moved irresolutely. She looked at Alex.

Peter had phoned Katrina that morning, asked her to come to meet Alex. She refused again. Outrage and protest at what he had done, his betrayal and treachery.

'What do you have to lose?' Peter had asked. In the end she hardly knew why she came.

There was Alex sitting between Peter and Lumy, and all three were looking at Katrina. It was as though she alone were judging Alex. As though Peter and Lumy were on his side, and they didn't care about her feelings of protest.

She dropped her eyes and looked at her hands. It was as good as though she had turned her back and walked away from them.

There was silence for a while. 'Shall we do Listening?' Lumy said at last.

'No,' Peter said slowly. 'I think we don't do Listening, until we can do it together.'

Katrina looked up at him in disbelief. She understood what was happening. Peter was saying that he and Lumy and Alex could Listen together, but she couldn't. He was excluding her from the group.

'Okay. Okay, let's all go out,' Alex said with forced heartiness. 'I'm buying dinner for you all.'

'Thank you, I don't have time,' Katrina said, standing up. 'I have to get home. Good night.'

'Don't go, Katrina. Come and join us,' said Lumy.

'No no. I have to go.'

'Stay on, Katrina,' said Peter.

'No no. Good night!'

She walked towards the door. Her legs carried her. Her mind drove her out of the room. Inside, a part of her was protesting: *Crazy! Why are you walking out on them? Why are you cutting yourself out of the group?* And she walked out of the well-known room where she had learned to Listen.

She walked out of the dim corridors of the house and out of the door. She stood on the gravel of the front drive, lit by adjacent streetlamps and the lights of neighbouring houses, under the faint stars of the hazy sky.

What am I doing? she asked herself. She didn't know what she wanted to do. Her main feeling was hurt pride, that had driven her out of the room. But something else was asking her why she was being so silly. She couldn't sort herself out. In confusion, she called: *Bezalia!*

I am here.

What am I doing, Bezalia!

You have walked out of the room. That is all.

Am I separated from the group?

Not in the least.

They want me to reconcile with Alex. I can't do it!

What do you have to lose?

Katrina saw herself again standing in front of Alex, to judge him, to punish him for hurting her. She did not want to step away from that stance. Did not want to give up the power to punish him.

You want to punish him, Katrina? You want to be revenged on him for hurting you?

Yes, that's what I want!

You want to punish him. Bezalia's voice was without condemnation. *This is why you walked out of the room, rather than give up his punishment.*

What can I do?

A smile. *You can go back into the room.*

Katrina stood hesitating in the night air outside the house. She'd feel like a fool, going back in again.

Put that on one side, Bezalia told her.

She would be saying it was all right, what Alex had done.

No. He admitted that he was wrong.

She would be forgiving him and letting him be reconciled with the group.

Yes. You too will be reconciled, after walking out on them.

Katrina found she was standing outside the door of the room. She wondered whether they had started Listening and whether she would walk into the middle of the session. She heard them talking inside. Someone said, 'The crabs are very big, for twenty-one dollars!' She turned the handle and went in.

They looked up and saw her and she felt a wave of happiness coming from them: unalloyed gladness from Peter and Lumy, plus considerable relief from Alex. She was amazed at how pleased they were to see her back, and it made easy the words that came to her lips: 'I just thought I didn't have to go home after all, I'd come back and join you.'

'Come in. Come and sit down,' Peter said, warmly and comfortingly, as though to someone who had just finished a hard struggle.

Alex gave her a most peculiar glance, a mixture of friendliness and sheepishness: *Have you forgiven me then?* She found herself smiling back at him.

She sat down between Lumy and Alex. And immediately Peter spoke the words which began their Listening. 'Listen to stillness. Listen to silence. Listen to the voice of your heart.'

Vacancy fell on them like darkness when a light is switched off. A huge stillness seized their minds and bodies and held them rapt. They rested: drifted in darkness, knowing only the presence of love.

Finally they emerged from their Listening and looked at each other with great contentment and fellowship. 'Come on now, let's go for dinner!' Alex insisted.

'I have something else to tell you,' Peter said. 'I've been doing some research—on China, on Mao's policies. I think I know what the dreams are about.'

'You can tell us in the restaurant,' Alex said, grabbing the handles of the wheelchair. 'They will give our table to someone else, if we don't get there in time.'

So it was in the sea-food restaurant, in the aqueous glow of the tanks of slow-swimming fish, in the fragrance of green tea and soya sauce, surrounded by white tablecloths and little dishes of peanuts and loud cheerful conversation, that Peter told his friends what he had learned about the famine that began in China in 1959.

Chapter Fourteen

At midnight, Cynthia shook Alex awake. 'Wake up! Lec, what are you dreaming, wake up!' Cynthia patted Alex's shoulder the way she patted Russell when he woke in the night.

'Lec, you have been having so many nightmares recently! Is it this Bezalia making you have bad dreams? You should ask Peter, can he help to take them away?'

Alex mumbled something. He did not want to tell Cynthia, that Peter said she herself had opened the door to the ongoing flow of dreams.

* * *

Peter dreamt of the white plain of misery. He was familiar with it now. He rolled his chair over the bumpy stones. *Goddam it, still in the chair, why can't I dream that I have my legs back!* The chill wind wailed like distant voices.

Vaporous shapes wavered in the mist. Skeletal figures that flickered and disappeared, as though they were trying to materialize and never quite making it. The wind moaned and howled and there seemed to be words in it.

'Speak louder! I can't hear you!' Peter cried. 'I can't see you!'

Shadowy figures took form. Starving people, all clavicles and jutting hipbones and toast-rack ribcages. The mournful voices hovered on the edge of audibility. *Feed us. Feed us.*

'You're dead!' Peter said to them. 'Why do the dead need to be fed?'

The voices moaned despairingly. *Feed us. Give us food.*

'Am I to give you rice and wheat?'

Give us, give us the food we need. Feed us.

The figures came closer, holding up bony hands in gestures of grief and suffering. They crowded around Peter. Their insubstantial bodies pressed all around him. Their voices of despair and need hissed in his ears.

Peter began to roll the chair. The figures melted as he rolled through them, dissolving back into mist. He was alone again on the road. All that was left was the feeling of despair, and the echo of voices. *Give us food. Feed us.*

Night after night, he saw the same skeletal figures with their weight of sorrow and bitter need. Their beggars' chorus began to haunt his waking thoughts. He had no idea how to give them what they wanted.

* * *

One evening Alex and Cynthia invited Peter to their place for dinner, and Cynthia's eldest brother Ronald, and his wife, Foo Choon, were there too. Cynthia told them that Peter said the source of her illness was in China, caused by the spirits of people who perished in the great famine. They nodded as though this sounded reasonable to them: a possible hypothesis.

'My friend Siok Phin's family,' said Foo Choon, 'after the grandmother died, the family started having bad luck. Their business lost money. Her brother fell off his motorbike. Then Siok Phin's sister dreamt about the grandmother. Grandmother said something was wrong with her grave. So, they called a feng-shui man to look at it. He said the next grave to that one was too high, it was throwing a shadow on grandmother's grave. In the end they put up a kind of screen on that side, a wall with marble columns, it looked quite okay. The grandmother came back to the daughter in another dream, she said she was satisfied with it.'

'Did they stop having bad luck?' Peter asked.

'Siok Phin said, after that one of the grandsons graduated top of his class!'

'Don't know whether it's really true!' Ronald laughed, neither believing nor disbelieving. 'So maybe we should take Cynthia to the feng-shui man or to the priests at the temple!'

'But we don't have any ancestors in China,' Cynthia said. 'We never had any family members who died in the famine.'

'I tell you what, it is hungry ghosts!' Foo Choon exclaimed. They all nodded again, except for Peter.

'I have heard of Hungry Ghosts Festival but I don't really know what it is about,' Peter said. 'At certain times of the year, I see these street entertainments, Chinese operas and those noisy auction sales, yelling very loud under my window late into the night!'

'The hungry ghosts are the spirits of people whose families don't make proper offerings to them at their graves. In the Seventh Month they come out and roam around and harm people. It is a very bad-luck time, you shouldn't have surgery or anything like that!' Foo Choon explained.

'There are a lot of ceremonies and prayers at this time, just to satisfy the ghosts and keep them happy,' Ronald said. 'The street operas are supposed to be for the ghosts to enjoy, not so much for the public.'

'I don't believe in all that,' Alex said, less pugnaciously than in the past. 'It's just superstition!'

'Who knows?' Ronald laughed tolerantly. 'Some of these big ceremonies, just a way to make money out of the people who attend the temple! For our family, no need to make so much fuss. We just observe some traditions in our own way.'

'We always observe *Cheng Beng*,' said Cynthia. 'That is about three weeks after Lunar New Year, Peter. We go to the cemeteries to visit the graves. Alex doesn't stop me from going.'

'I won't dare to stop you!' Alex said, pretending to look scared of her. 'Hey, have we got any beer in the fridge? Anybody want some?'

Over the beer, they stated their various ideas about what would happen to people's souls after death. Even Alex, following the church's hard line that pagan souls went straight to hell, thought it was possible that unrestful souls might return to earth to trouble the living.

Cynthia told Peter about the ritual that in their dialect was called Cheng Beng. In old China at the beginning of spring, the people went out to the countryside to see the new green and visit the ancestral graves. In seasonless Singapore, Cynthia's family still celebrated the yearly Festival of Spring Brightness.

Ronald, as the eldest of his generation, would phone around and organize the family. A decade ago, they went out in strings of cars, in recent years Ronald had just hired an air-conditioned bus for all of them. There were twenty-nine living descendants of their grandfather, his four sons, and their seven wives. Subtract those who couldn't make the date, add in spouses and children, and the bus would be pretty full. They would assemble at Ronald's place early in the morning and board the bus with a lot of chatter and merriment and remarks on how children had grown.

The first site to visit was always the grandfather's grave at Lim Chu Kang. From the carpark they threaded the narrow paths to the grave, which was an old-fashioned semi-circular hearth. Labourers had already cut the grass, the family inspected the work and took note of any needed repairs.

The offerings were laid out. There were red candles, a pile of oranges, three cups of tea. There were dishes of cooked food. Cynthia's unmarried sister brought a bowl of vinegared pig's feet, as her mother had done every year, saying this had been the grandfather's favourite dish; although the grandfather had died before Alice was born.

Incense sticks were lit. First Ronald, then each descendant, bowed in front of the grave, each waved incense sticks and raised a cup of tea in both hands to the sky. Most of them bowed silently, the action of respect was all that was needed, but Alice as she bowed, sang out a long, improvised chant. She told the grandfather that his children had come to honour him; she sang out their various names and asked him to send them good fortune. 'Listen to her, she mourns as well as our mother used to do,' the family said admiringly.

The offerings were packed away and the family bustled back into the bus, to visit two other cemeteries where other ancestors were buried. After the last visit they found a shady pavilion and sat down for lunch. The children ran around with their cousins, the adults rested and ate the pig's feet and other food off plastic plates.

Cynthia always enjoyed the family celebration of Cheng Beng. It was nice to get together with relatives whom you seldom saw. It was nice to get out for a day of sunshine and fresh air. The wind blew over the open fields of the cemeteries, carrying smells of incense and cut grass. The avenue of trumpet-flower trees at Lim Chu Kang was in bloom, lifting clouds of white blossom against the blue sky.

'So, Peter! You are Indian, but you believe in this, eh?' asked Ronald. 'You think that maybe some ghosts from China have caught hold of Cynthia!'

'Do you know about that famine in China, in 1959?' said Peter. He told the story again, and they went through the same horror and indignation.

'I say, man,' Ronald commented, 'those ghosts really must be damn sore. Suffering like that. Their own people making them suffer. They must be bloody angry.'

Foo Choon nodded. 'And some more, they did not have any proper funerals.'

'Right after the Great Leap Forward came the Cultural Revolution,' Peter said. 'Religion was banned as feudal superstition. So you're right, nobody ever said prayers for those dead. No one was even allowed to mention their deaths.'

'No wonder they are angry. So maybe somehow, they caught hold of our Cynthia! Better take her to the temple!'

'Cynthia, tomorrow we go to the temple to see the priest,' said Foo Choon. 'Maybe he will know what to do.'

'Ask him whether he can say prayers for the people who died in China,' said Peter.

A few days later Cynthia reported that the priest at the temple had agreed to conduct a special ritual for her. 'He chanted some prayers over me, just like your church elders did. But when I asked whether it was spirits from China he shook his head. I don't think he knew anything about it. And I have lost another half-kilo since last month.'

* * *

Alex and his friends continued to dream.

Katrina, sleeping, saw a white plain. Fumes of sorrow and despair rose to a stormy sky above. There were ruinous houses with upturned eaves. The ground was littered with skeletal remains and ragged bodies, half-decomposed.

This dream had been repeating, in various forms, ever since the first session with Cynthia. Usually Katrina just dreamed of the white plain and felt depressed all through the next day. But once or twice there was a variation to the dream.

In the sky above rode Bezalia, Lady of the Winds. Her white robes blew, the tempest roared around her. She heard the sound of many voices, the cry of those who suffered, in sighs and moans and endless weeping. Riding the storm-dragon, she swooped down towards the plain.

Lightning slashed through the clouds. It blasted through Bezalia. Her body convulsed. She screamed, louder than the howl of wind. She flung her hands wide, sparks streaming from each finger, and her head was surrounded by a great bush as each long hair stood away from the rest. She recovered, to stand poised again on the crown of the plunging beast, with the lightning bolts crackling around her.

The dragon soared and writhed through the clouds and the lightning struck again and again. Bezalia hung transfixed by torrents of voltage streaming between earth and sky.

The dream would end with this terrible and disturbing image, of Bezalia letting the lightning strike through her body: making of herself a conduit, the interface between earth and heaven.

Katrina would snap awake with her heart pounding. What she felt was not fear but a kind of excitement, as though she had seen something very wonderful.

* * *

'Have you seen today's paper, Alex?' Peter said on the phone. 'The doctors say they've recognized that Cynthia has a new disease—okay she's out, tell her when she comes in—no, they can't cure it yet, don't get too hopeful. They still don't know anything, except that other people have suffered the same thing. They call it Unexplained Weight Loss Syndrome.'

'They don't know how to cure it?'

'I'm afraid not. They found that there have been several cases in Singapore over the past six years, only the cases weren't recognized as a separate disease.'

'Just like Cynthia? People getting thinner and thinner and weaker?'

'Yes. Maybe now they can do more research, find out what those people had in common.'

'So, what happened to those earlier cases? Did they recover?'

Peter hesitated. 'You'd better read the newspaper,' he said.

'What's it called again?'

'The newspaper headline called it "Famine Syndrome".'

The report said nine cases had been identified in Singapore. In the past four years, three had died in hospital, two were in hospital and four more were still living at home.

The newspapers kept the victims' names confidential, but the details soon spread through society grapevines.

'I know one of them!' Lumy told her friends, 'Jason Cheong, my mother's cousin's grandson, such a clever boy, is he sick? I must go and visit him.'

'Ask him if he ever dreamt of China,' Peter said.

Lumy, carrying cake and fruit and health drinks, went to the hospital. Lumy's cousin greeted her warmly, grateful for her visit, and told her about all the tests and treatments the doctors had tried in vain. Jason's father told his worries about the costs and the consequences of the illness on Jason's future. The private ward was crowded with new clothes, games, and electronic devices, to distract Jason during his hospital stay. Jason, in a trendy sports windcheater over his hospital pyjamas, looked up unwillingly from his computer game and told Lumy that he slept well, had no bad dreams, had never dreamt of China.

A group of Jason's friends came in. Jason was surrounded by noisy teenagers, looking at his screen. The video game was about zombies slaughtering humans and being slaughtered—cruelty and death and the afterlife turned into gaming points to fuel the children's excitement and mirth. Lumy watched them, the giggling girls and bickering boys, and the emaciated boy in the bed, and thought of the warm seas around Singapore, teeming with tiny life. All drawing nutrient from the same waters, and if some harmful substance entered the sea, eventually the whole ocean knew about the pollution, but it was the weakest, most vulnerable ones which would perish first. She seemed to see the children and the anxious parents as small creatures unaware of the great spiritual realm they swam in, knowing nothing outside their own tiny selves. In their ignorance they had no defences, would not recognize any toxic contamination. *Poor things,* Lumy thought to herself, *poor poor things!*

Chapter Fifteen

Alex was talking to Miss Lee about an incoming shipment of tiles. Suddenly the office seemed to darken around him. He felt a cramp in his gut and an aching emptiness inside. In a moment the feeling passed, leaving him blinking at bright sunlight and Miss Lee's concerned face. 'Nothing!' Alex said, 'I'm all right!' although he felt shaken and momentarily disorientated. Later that day the same thing happened again: a flash of disconnected sensation, bothering his daily life.

Katrina felt cold. She heard far-off wailing and something pale passed in front of her eyes: a small greyish thing with thin projections. Terrible misery flooded over her. In the midst of a meeting, she was swept away from her surroundings, and she came back to find she had stopped halfway through a presentation, and Khoon Huat was glaring at her as though to say she should be sick on her own time, not on his.

She had gained enough aplomb to stay calm at having made a spectacle of herself; she apologized and got on with her talk, brushing aside the horror that lingered at the back of her mind. *What was that?* she wondered when she had time. She could find no answer, but it happened again and again.

* * *

Intermittently, as though carried to him by gusting wind, Peter heard the chorus of pleading voices. *Feed us.* He sat at his desk and saw the shambling figures, felt their desperate, sorrowful appeal.

Where have I felt something like that before? He searched his memory. *Where was it?*

He remembered three sullen children, the son and daughters of a distant cousin of Peter's family. The man was an eminent doctor, prosperous and respected. Later there were shockwaves of shame and horror through the clan, when they found out that the doctor had regularly brutalized his children when they were small.

Peter had felt the same frustrated despair from the doctor's children when he met them during their abused childhood. They had a secret that they dared not tell. They were living a lie that destroyed their own inner truth. In school they lied and stole. Peter had felt their anger at the whole world, turned inward in self-hatred.

That is the feeling. The poison of truth suppressed. The despair of living a lie.

The mist swirled and hid the dim figures, the wind drowned their voices, and they cried their frustration that only he could hear.

* * *

Lumy saw nothing, heard nothing: just felt weakness throughout her body, her limbs aching, heart pounding and head spinning dizzily. It happened when she was driving down the BKE and she came back to a blare of horns, found she had drifted onto the soft shoulder and slowed to a near stop. She put on the handbrake and waited to recover herself, shaken as much by the near-crash as by the strange feelings.

What was that, Bezalia? I never felt anything like that in my life—where did it come from? Is it from the people who suffered in China?

Yes. It is from the people who suffered starvation.

So pitiful, said Lumy. She sat behind the wheel of her car, gazing at the green depths of jungle on either side of the BKE, and thought of people who had eaten no full meal for a month; who felt what she had felt all the time, every day till they died. *So terrible for them,* she said with tears in her eyes. It was a while before she drove on, feeling gloomy and sad; with a sorrow that originated not from some distant source, but in her own compassionate heart.

* * *

Alex was having several of those episodes each day: a wave of emotions and a rush of indecipherable images, leaving him shaken and confused.

What's happening, Bezalia? Am I going crazy or what? I feel like I'm losing my mind!

They can't harm you, Alex. Just listen and try to hear what is being said to you.

I don't know what it's about! I can't make head or tail of these flashes!

Wait till clarity comes.

You always say 'wait, Bezalia!'

Laughter. *And you always want the answers now, now, now!*

Cynthia wants me to go to see Dr Chng. Now she's the one who's worrying about me! But Dr Chng would just give me tranquilizers. Or he would think I'm going nuts.

If you go to the doctor, it is only in order to run around and be busy, to escape from the pain.

Of course I want to escape from the pain! What else is there to do?

A smile. *Endurance. Bear with the pain. Listen.*

Before bedtime Alex sat and Listened: and the horrible emotions which had flashed through him during the day came welling up. Waves of horror and rage and guilt swept over his head. He gulped and breathed deeply and, as he had been taught, kept on repeating his Bible word. The wave of agitation washed over him, peaked, slowly ebbed away. It was gone, and he continued listening to his word, with a sense of relief.

'Me too,' Peter said when Alex related this, 'I think Listening is the only thing that's keeping me sane.'

They were meeting almost every day to discuss what they were going through, like members of some special support group. 'I don't dare to drive anymore,' said Lumy, 'I'm taking taxi to go around town. Alex, be careful when you are driving!'

'I can't concentrate on my work,' said Katrina.

'I've been very irritable,' said Peter. 'Like I've got our SSD Chairman on the phone, old Mr Khoo, he's droning on and on, and I just want him to shut up and go away. I have acid in my stomach all the time.'

'Doctor says my HBP is up again,' said Lumy.

'Prozac doesn't help,' said Katrina. 'I get the flashbacks once or twice each day. I hear someone wailing and crying. I see this pale thing moving, grey-blue, like a small starfish . . . and I have such a pain in my heart . . . '

'I asked my parish priest to say a Mass for the dead,' Peter said.

'It hasn't worked yet!' said Katrina. 'Maybe,' she said jokingly, 'we should all be going to the temples and churches.'

'I did ask Bezalia whether we should do that,' said Peter.

'What did she say?'

'Wait and Listen.'

* * *

One evening they were sitting round Lumy's dining table with the television playing, with bowls of red-bean drink in front of them. They had switched on the television to catch some announcement about the road-pricing scheme, and they left it on while they ate. In the midst of their chat they saw that Peter was watching the screen intently; he gestured to Lumy to turn up the sound.

His attention had been caught by an image of candleflames in darkness, and mournful music, sorrowfully echoing. 'At Auschwitz,' said the voice-over, 'those who died in the Holocaust are remembered.'

A black-clad, silver-bearded man chanted prayers. A group of mourners lit candles at a dark stone monument.

'For a long time, we did not admit this thing,' said a woman interviewed on a Hamburg street. 'We denied that it happened.'

The screen showed images of the Holocaust and clips documenting the slow change in Germany, from denial to the admission of collective responsibility.

'It's good that the guilt is recognized,' said a man in the sunlight of Israel. Then it was night, and hundreds of people stood in silence, holding candles.

The program broke for a commercial. Alex asked, 'What's this all about?'

Lumy fetched the newspaper. Katrina read, 'This is a program called Remembering the Past, focusing on war memories in Germany and Japan.'

'I know it's something very important for us,' said Peter.

Katrina said, 'I don't know any Jews. Never met any. But when we see such shows, we do feel very sorry for what happened to them.'

The program resumed. Old wartime footage: a street in China, crowds fleeing from gunfire. There were interviews with elderly people who remembered being there, in Nanking in 1939. A Japanese minister said that the Rape of Nanking did not happen. A spokesman in Shanghai called for the Japanese to recognize their guilt. The documentary was targeting the Japanese for denial of responsibility, their failure to admit that the atrocity ever happened. With muted music, suggesting lingering pain and resentment, the screen showed commemoration candles being lit in Nanking.

At the next break Lumy said, 'I remember when the Japs occupied Singapore. My mother kept us at home, she wouldn't let us go out in the street.'

Alex grew heated with inherited grievance. 'They took my grandfather away and shot him! Till this day my grandmother has never forgiven them!'

'Thirty years later, my uncles were telling me stories about the war,' said Peter. 'They talked about it till it became a sort of after-dinner story. The pain's faded by repetition over the years.'

The last segment of the program went to Ireland, where Catholics and Protestants gathered to remember all who had died in the Troubles. Families of people who had been killed on both sides of the conflict, brought gifts and flowers to lay at a memorial stone.

A long-haired, bearded tenor played a guitar and sang. *It's time for healing, it's time for forgiving. Time to confess, to be reconciled.* By the light of a thousand candles, a huge crowd wept and cheered and sang together. *Light up the darkness, mend the world.*

The song repeated as the credits rolled. 'Producer, Tony Li,' Katrina read, 'Hong Kong Eravision.'

Alex said, 'Terrible, these Japanese! Still never say sorry for what they did.'

Peter disregarded their talk. 'Now I know what we have to do,' he said intensely. 'We have to go to China and find the graves of people who died in the famine. We have to light candles on their graves.'

* * *

At first the trip to China was not a certain thing. 'I'm sorry. I can't say that you all must go to China,' Peter said on second thoughts. 'For me, I feel compelled. I feel I have to go.'

Lumy said cheerfully, 'I'll come with you. I have toured in the southern provinces, but I've never visited Henan. Alex, you come also, and Katrina! Travelling in China will be easier, with more people to help!'

Katrina hesitated. 'I don't know. I have ten days' leave left this year. I was planning to go to Brisbane and the Gold Coast.'

Peter looked at Katrina and Alex. 'Haven't you felt the misery of those unhappy souls?'

Alex nodded but looked very doubtful. 'Yes, well, if I go, will Cynthia get better?'

Peter shook his head. 'I have no idea! I'm not thinking of this as some kind of pilgrimage, seeking a miracle cure, we light the candles and Cynthia immediately recovers. It is something to be done, for the sake of those who suffer: I don't know about any other effects.'

'Then maybe I should stay here at home and take care of Cynthia!'

'I know there are troubled spirits,' Katrina admitted. She looked at Lumy standing behind Peter's wheelchair. She should offer to help them, she thought unwillingly: a cripple and an elderly woman travelling to China, neither of them speaking Putonghua. She said loudly, 'Why do any of us have to go? Those people have been dead for thirty-five years! Okay they suffered, they're crying—what's that got to do with us? Why don't we just refuse to listen to them?'

Katrina saw the others looking at her. The room had gone very quiet. She heard her own words loud in the silence: *Why don't we just refuse to listen to them?*

Listening is what you have been called to do, Bezalia said. They all heard her voice clearly in their hearts, as definite as an auditory sensation. *You have all let it enlarge you, change you, bring you closer to God within you. You don't know how happy it makes me, to see what you have become! I feel so proud, as I watch you grow.*

Katrina's eyes filled with tears as the words rang in her mind.

*If you make this trip to China, you will fulfil more of what you could
be. My dear ones, you have been offered this chance to help to heal the world.
Do it, for the sake of what I love in you.*

'Did I get it right, Bezalia, what I propose to do?' Peter asked.

*Yes, Peter. You need to go to the place of greatest suffering and make
reparation there.*

Where do we have to go? Katrina asked. What exactly do we
have to do?

*Against the death of thirty million there is nothing that you can do. Just
be there. Be the link, to bring love to the wounded land.*

Bezalia's presence was gone. At last Alex said, 'I will come to
China. I can speak Putonghua. I'll help to push the chair.'

'I'm willing to come,' Katrina said. 'But where are we going to
find the graves? Somewhere in Henan county? Where in Henan?
Bezalia didn't tell us!'

Peter smiled wryly. 'Katrina, you're the one that's going to
tell us! Where's my case, Lumy? I have a big map of the area . . .
Thanks. See, I have this large-scale map of Henan county, I got
it from the Chinese Embassy in Dalvey Road. Come over here,
Katrina . . . '

'No,' said Katrina, guessing what Peter intended. She was full
of panic. 'No way!'

'I want you to take this pencil and make a mark at random on
the map,' Peter said with gentle firmness. 'Don't think about it,
don't go all cerebral on me, just do it!'

'I don't want to do it! It's all nonsense!'

'Don't be scared!' Lumy encouraged. 'Just give it a try,
just *gasak*!'

'No! I won't do it!'

Peter put down the pencil he'd been holding out to her. 'Okay.
Okay. Take it easy!'

'Have a drink,' said Lumy, 'have some more *angtowsuay*.'

'I don't believe in this psychic stuff! It's so irrational! It doesn't make sense!'

'And that scares you?' said Peter. 'Because you can't understand it, you can't control it?'

Katrina nodded in surprise. 'Yeah, that's it, how did you know?'

Peter laughed easily. 'I also hate being powerless! But that desire for control, it's just another bit of emotional junk we have to learn to throw away! So, Katrina, are you ready to give it a go? Dare to act without certain knowledge. Just strike out boldly, as Lumy says. Give it a try.'

Katrina approached reluctantly. 'You mean to say, wherever I pick out on the map, that's where we buy our tickets for?'

Alex chimed in. 'No harm in trying! Even if you are right or wrong, how will we ever know!'

'Thanks very much!' grumbled Katrina, 'now you say we'll never know if I'm right!'

'There's no right or wrong. No penalty for success or failure!' Peter laughed, putting the pencil in her hand. 'Close your eyes!'

'Wait a minute!' said Katrina. 'We're all in this together, right? We're all like one unified body called to this task? So why am I the only one playing Treasure Hunt?'

'Because you're the one who has shown signs of psychic knowledge.'

'Nope! If I've got to do it, the rest of you do it too.'

The project turned into a kind of game. Each of them approached the map and stabbed the pencil down at random. Alex's first attempt landed in a lake, to laughter and wisecracks. Each made three attempts.

Lumy and Alex made widely scattered marks on the map. Peter's attempts bracketed the county capital of Zhengzhou. *Maybe that's where the lies were thickest,* he thought. And Katrina's three attempts: 'All quite close together, in a small triangle,' said

Lumy. 'And if you take the centre of the triangle . . . what's that town?'

Alex and Katrina read the Chinese characters. 'A town called Chengshen.'

* * *

'I'll try to get the bank to sponsor our airfares,' Peter reflected. 'I'd like to have more people involved in this project of reconciliation.'

'You think the bank will help you make offerings to hungry ghosts?' Katrina asked incredulously.

Peter grinned. 'Eric Lee goes back a long way with me . . . I'm thinking, if we have some contact with Singapore's financial and banking sector, that's like really touching the corporate soul of Singapore! If we get sponsorship from the bank—it's like we're tapping into the spiritual energy of three million Singaporeans!'

Katrina stared at him. 'Are you serious?'

Peter laughed light-heartedly. 'Hey, Kats, this whole enterprise is crazy, we just gotta go with it and fly! My god, it feels good to have a plan, a direction in which to move, after all these weeks of not knowing.'

'I'll apply for leave,' Katrina said. 'Ten days should be enough to just go there and come back. Maybe I can spend some time in Hong Kong on the way back!'

'Alex, Lumy, can you arrange to go away?' said Peter. 'I tell you something. I have found that when you have been called to do something, when it's what you are meant to be doing, all the paths open up for you.'

Lumy nodded. 'Yes, I have really experienced this you know! When you do what God is telling you to do, everything becomes very easy for you, and you will have no obstacles, and all the difficulties just clear up by themselves!'

Peter added, 'That helps to confirm that you are on the right path.'

* * *

Katrina applied for leave. May Lee in the next room was looking for a way to go to Chicago next spring and was eager to agree to cover for Katrina if Katrina would do the same for her.

Alex discussed it with Cynthia. She said that her sister was renting a bungalow in Cameron Highlands for a month during the school holidays. She had asked Cynthia to come along with Alex and Russell, but Cynthia had thought Alex would have found that kind of holiday too tedious. It would be fine for Cynthia and Russell to go, while Alex went to China.

* * *

Their trip to China was organized. Eric Lee came forth with sponsorship for tickets. Lumy's travel agent got their tickets and their visas for China. Everything went smoothly till they boarded the SIA flight for Hong Kong.

BOOK THREE

After Dongshandu

Chapter Sixteen

'Road broken!' cried the driver, in the thick accent they could barely understand. A crowd of people surrounded the bus, and the words were repeated many times: 'Road broken!'

When they reached Zhengzhou, they had planned to rent a car and drive to the village of Chengshen. They had the addresses of two rental agencies. Both agencies refused to let their cars be driven beyond the city. The next morning, they went to the bus station and boarded a long-distance bus. They were told that in three days the bus would bring them to Chengshen.

They endured a day's travel in the bus. They sat on uncushioned wooden seats, while the wheelchair was tied on the roof next to a coop of chickens. The bus was crowded with travellers all talking loudly over the constant blare of the bus driver's choice of music, while the bus jolted over uneven roads deep into the countryside, across the plain and into the hills.

In the afternoon of the second day, the bus stopped in a tiny village and made no further progress. The Singaporeans understood at last that the road ahead was blocked by a landslide, and the bus would not go on that day.

'How can they do this! What nonsense is this!' Alex heard his own voice rising angrily. He felt his face flushing and his breath growing tight in his chest. He saw the passengers and the local people, standing in a crowd around the bus. Their faces looked mean and sly, with leering mouths and narrowed, squinting eyes.

He saw Lumy looking at him with an expression of concern, and Katrina with irritated resignation, and Peter gazing at him quietly: as though he were waiting to see what Alex would do.

Alex noticed something like a film before his eyes. He seemed to be peering at these people through a kind of screen, and now he realized that there were distortions in his vision which were in the screen, not in reality. For a strange moment, he saw two scenes at once: the ugly, hostile crowd of his paranoia, and a bunch of peasants who were ordinary people. And he saw there were two ways he could act.

Bezalia spoke without words in his heart. *You can get angry, and yell and shout and upset everybody before you do whatever needs to be done. Or you can just go on and start dealing with the problem right away.*

It did not seem as though he had to make a big decision. He said quietly to the bus driver, 'Friend, can you tell me, when will the road be clear? When can we go on?' Eventually, he went back to his friends and reported, 'Nobody knows when the road can be cleared!'

'Maybe we should look for a place to sleep tonight,' Lumy said.

'We gonna spend the night here?' Alex said. 'Yeah, it's not like Singapore, just phone up to PWD and the road will be cleared in a few hours! You are right. Everybody would be looking for a place to sleep. Is there any hotel in this place?'

They found accommodation, in the end, in the village, in the local eating-shop. A big room had been divided by a wooden partition. In the larger portion were the cooking area and tables for customers, with a radio constantly playing. The smaller division was used as a store, piled with sacks and boxes. Along one wall ran a brick sleeping-platform, with a fireplace underneath.

The owner of the eating shop readily agreed to take in the travellers. Katrina grinned, watching him busily directing his family members to clear space on the sleeping-platform and light a fire under it. 'He's looking at overseas Chinese and he's getting yuan signs in his eyes! But just one room—are we all going to sleep together?'

'Never mind, for one night only,' Lumy replied.

In the cold winter evening, they stood outside the shop, looking at the village of Nanchiao. The village consisted of two rows of low houses. Many had front portions built of planks and brick and concrete; at the back were older, shabby sections made of mud bricks. Outside one house they saw something that looked very familiar to the Singaporeans: a small board set upright, painted red and covered with lines of black characters, with a jar of incense sticks standing in front. It was an altar to the spirits of heaven and earth.

'See, religion is making a come-back,' Katrina said.

Peter nodded. 'Remember we saw that brand-new temple in Zhengzhou?'

'During the Cultural Revolution, people would probably have been executed for putting up an altar like this,' said Alex. 'Now they are allowed to do it!'

Lines of plastic shelters stood in the bare fields around them. The fields stretched endlessly, fields that had been cultivated far back in time. They were surrounded by land enough for sixty Singapore islands; a past stretching back for sixty times Singapore's history.

Beside the dusty road grew scattered bushes decked with bright coloured flags, it seemed, gaily fluttering in the wind. 'Prayer slips, maybe,' Peter said, 'like in Tibet and Nepal.'

Looking closer they saw that the fluttering scraps were discarded plastic bags, hundreds of them, caught in the leafless branches of the trees, rustling in the wind. All along the edges of the road were scraps of paper and plastic and various kinds of trash.

Beyond the road were brown hills covered in grass and shrubs. 'No forests,' Katrina remarked.

'They were cut down for firewood,' Peter said. 'In Mao's Great Leap Forward, the people were ordered to make steel in small-scale backyard furnaces. The people gathered all the iron in the village to melt for scrap. They took their hoes and plough blades, the woks from the kitchens. They took down their doors and windows, to use the hinges and bolts as scrap and the wood as fuel. They felled the trees for firewood so now the hills are bare.'

'Wood-fire furnaces, to make steel?' Alex asked, marvelling. 'Did they get good results?'

'Nope. 'Peter's voice sounded tired. 'They melted their iron and produced worthless spongy metal. It could not be used for anything.'

'Steel furnaces with wood fuel, doesn't sound as though it would work!' Alex repeated. 'Did they have some new technology to try?'

'Mao did not believe in technology. He did not believe in modern scientific methods. He said the peasants were going to do what science said couldn't be done. They would succeed just by the sheer effort of will.'

'That's crazy!' Katrina said.

'The people threw their hearts into following Mao's vision. He dreamed of the socialist miracle; they died in pursuing it. North of Zhengzhou, there's the famous Red Flag Canal. It was meant to prove that China's people could conquer the physical world, without Western science.'

Katrina remembered reading about it. 'The guidebook says tunnels were hewed through the mountain. Hundreds of dams were built, miles of canals. The work was done by hand, without the help of engineers and machines.'

'Millions of people laboured. Thousands of them died,' Peter said wearily. They don't put that in the guidebooks. Look, it's nearly dark, it's getting damned cold. Let's go inside and do our Listening. And then I want to sleep, I'm shattered.'

Lumy looked at the lines of pain on Peter's face. 'This long bus journey is terrible, huh!'

'I'll be okay, I'll take two Percodan and turn in early. We're not very far from Chengshen now. If the road's clear, we should reach it tomorrow.'

They slept in a line on the kang, enjoying the tiny warmth from the fire beneath the bricks, wrapped in the questionable blankets on top of all their clothes.

* * *

Next morning, they ate steamed buns in the eating-shop. They walked round the village again. They asked the driver of the bus when he thought the road might be cleared; he didn't know. There seemed to be nothing to do but to return to the shop and wait for it to be time for lunch. And then nothing to do in the afternoon but wait for it to be time for dinner; and they had soon found that the food was nothing to look forward to, coarse and bland to their taste. Even the rice the villagers ate seemed to have an unpleasant taste and smell.

Next day there was no news of the road being repaired, and they began to realize they might have to stay for some time, in this village where the people were totally unused to foreigners. People would come into the storeroom where the visitors were staying, to take a look at the strangers. Alex complained that he could not even go to the primitive unenclosed toilet without being stared at: 'Like they have to see whether our shit is the same as theirs!'

'They really don't know what other people are like,' agreed Peter. He and his wheelchair were the chief target of the villagers' curiosity.

'They stare at us like we are animals in the zoo,' said Katrina. She saw themselves in a cage, with the villagers looking in from the other side of the bars.

Peter said, 'Bezalia says that we should go towards them, we should step through the bars.'

They called a 'press conference,' as Katrina termed it, a 'meet-the–people session,' Alex said. Word went out that the visitors were inviting everyone to drink tea in the eating shop, and the whole village turned up.

Alex delivered the speech which they had all helped to prepare. He expressed the travellers' admiration for the fine village of Nanchiao, and their gratitude for help in their difficulty. He introduced himself and his friends.

Lumy stepped forward, exotic in her makeup and jewelry and smart travelling suit. She beamed at the village people as she'd have smiled at an assembly of Singapore's social stars. She spoke in her native Hokkien, and Alex translated. 'I come from Singapore. I am sixty-four years old. I have a husband in Singapore who is a businessman. I have two sons and a daughter, and four grandchildren. My sons work in America.'

She went on with more details about herself and her family. 'Don't tell them how different Singapore is from China,' Peter had advised, 'tell them things they can connect to.' The villagers listened with deep attention. Katrina could see the dividing bars disappearing, as they realized the visitors were really people like themselves.

Katrina introduced herself next, knowing that she could not help making a speech like a formal office presentation. Despite her efforts to smile and make eye-contact, she did not connect to the people as much as Lumy had done.

Peter rolled his chair forward. 'Ni hou ma?' he said. The villagers' attention peaked. Peter explained through translation that he belonged to an ethnic minority in Singapore, and that he had been injured in an accident fifteen years ago. Their intense curiosity felt like an invasive probe, which he had to force himself to allow, to accept into himself. He gave a short version of his usual 'Cripple's Lib' speech, proclaiming that disabled people, with the support of their friends, could have satisfying and useful lives. As a climax, the people were invited to examine the wheelchair. They all surged forward to crowd around the chair and Alex was just in time to politely fend them off, till Peter could be moved into another seat.

The tea-party proceeded with a hubbub of cheerful chatter. There were many pots of tea. The eating-shop had provided trays of sweet cakes. Local headmen talked to the visitors: the school teacher, the political officer, the elders of the Chang clan to which most of the village belonged. 'Why are you going to Chengshen?' asked the teacher.

Alex had not mentioned this subject in his introduction. They had decided to mention the famine as little as possible, as the subject would be unpopular with the Chinese government. 'We are going to Chengshen to pray at some graves. We are going to make grave offerings.'

The headmen took this with hardly a blink. Alex remembered the little altar they had seen. 'Ah. Is it the grave of your ancestor?' asked the teacher.

'No,' Alex replied, 'it's the grave of persons who died in 1960.'

'Ah huh, ah huh,' the teacher assented mildly. His face had gone bland and expressionless. So had the faces of the people around him. Katrina could feel the shockwave spreading through them.

'Do you know the names of the dead?' asked the political officer.

'Their name was Chang,' Alex replied just as blandly, knowing that Chang was the name of just about every household in the village.

The school teacher smiled and changed the subject and asked what business Alex did in Singapore.

Chapter Seventeen

They had been four days in the village. On the second day, the bus had returned to Zhengzhou. They wrote faxes to Singapore for the bus driver to send from Zhengzhou.

'We should go back with the bus,' Alex said. 'Wait in Zhengzhou till the road is clear.'

'No,' said Peter. 'We'll stay here.'

'Why? So dull here, so boring, the food is lousy!'

'Do you have a strong reason for going back to Zhengzhou?' Peter said. 'We started this trip. We don't turn back without some serious reason. Anyway, you didn't like the food in Zhengzhou either!'

'I still have lots of *sambal blachan*,' Lumy said. With the addition of her eye-wateringly hot and pungent shrimp paste, they could swallow the bland food.

'But how long will it take to clear the road?' Katrina asked. 'What if it takes weeks?'

'We stay here,' said Peter.

'I took two weeks' leave. I thought that would be more than enough,' Katrina said worriedly.

'Don't worry about your leave,' Lumy said. 'I sent a fax to Chan Leong, I asked him to speak to your boss Khoon Huat.' Katrina stared. She tended to forget that Lumy had access to the power-structures in Singapore.

Peter was quiet, rubbing his forehead. *I feel lousy, Bezalia. My back aches like hell. This village street, these fields look so dull and dreary to me.*

A sympathetic brush of fingers on his cheek. *Yes, Peter. You feel the sorrow of the land. You are not very far away from Chengshen. This place also suffered the famine.*

* * *

The days in Nanchiao passed slowly. One day, Alex learned there was a village seven miles away, where they had a bigger shop than the one in Nanchiao. He borrowed a bicycle and made a shopping trip. He sent some faxes and came back loaded with groceries. He guessed the sizes and triumphantly brought back warm socks and sweaters and even woolly hats, to present to his friends.

Other days, Alex spent his time walking around the village. People stared at him, and he stared back at them. He talked to them, answered the repeated questions, asked questions of his own about the activities he saw. He learned the names of many villagers. He became acquainted with many; he did not feel that he knew anyone.

Funny, I'm surrounded by all these people, but I still feel alone. He rejoined his friends for the mid-day meal and then he walked around some more, talking to villagers, always an outsider. *Funny, I feel alone, but I don't feel lonely.*

Katrina went out walking every day. Six fast kilometres every morning; she would go home in great shape after all this exercise. The local women stared at her in amazement. She compared herself with the women of her own age, who looked ten years older. They plodded around their fields, carrying loads she could not have lifted, while she trotted lightly around in her Reeboks, burning energy just to stay slim and keep fit. When she tried to talk to them she felt they regarded her as an alien among them.

She trotted briskly through the cold dry fields. *Bezalia, Lady of the Winds, are you here in this barren place?*

I am here. I hear the cry that goes up from these fields. This is the place to which you were called.

* * *

Peter's wheelchair could not roll on the uneven, stony paths. He spent the days sitting on the heated sleeping-platform. He wrapped himself in all his clothes and asked Lumy to open the wooden shutters of the window, letting in cold air and light and a view of the village and the fields beyond.

The dry corncobs and stalks that burned in the fireplace produced much smoke and little heat. On the other side of the wooden partition the radio played all day, and people talked loudly in the eating-shop. He tried to read or write but he could not shut out the sounds. His head ached from the effort to concentrate. He could not think.

So, he stopped trying to think and listened to the sounds. He let them wash through his mind and fill him. He sat relaxed, and amidst the noise he found the place of silence.

* * *

Lumy sat all day in the eating-shop. Chatting in Hokkien, she got to know the Chang family: the father, the two sons, the mother, the old grandmother, and the widow they called Sixth Aunt, who lived with them.

She helped the women with their cooking. With delight she learned to make noodles: to mix flour and water, to knead and roll and cut and boil.

She served her noodles to her friends, saying, 'At home we always buy our noodles in packets from the market! It's nice to make them ourselves!' Alex, slurping them up with enthusiasm, fully appreciated this primordial satisfaction.

Katrina bit into crunchy cabbage and added, 'And these vegetables are grown in the fields right here, not brought into some supermarket!!'

'And they are fertilized with our very own shit,' Peter said, deadpan, letting Katrina yelp and grimace in disgust.

'Don't worry! I washed the vegetables. I washed them very carefully,' Lumy assured her.

'I watch the old man growing them,' said Peter. 'All day he's in and out of those little shelters, tending the vegetables.'

'He's got vegetables and beans and cucumbers growing in those shelters, under heavy plastic sheeting,' said Alex. 'At night he covers them up to keep them warm. You see those big rolls of matting on the roofs. Every morning at dawn, he's climbing up there to roll up the covers. When it gets dark, he's carefully letting them down.'

'His vegetables are like his babies,' said Lumy.

'He picks off insects, he waters them, and fertilizes them,' Katrina said.

Alex laughed. 'Once I saw him hurrying across the field to reach the toilet. He could have done his business anywhere in the fields. But he had to reach his toilet so that he could keep the stuff to use for fertilizer.'

'That old farmer must have been here in 1959,' said Peter. 'When the peasants were forced to start using Mao's new farming methods. One method was deep ploughing, they were ordered to cut their furrows twelve feet deep.'

'Twelve feet deep? Two times a man's height?' Alex repeated. 'You need bulldozers for that!'

'They did it all by hand, with wooden tools since the iron ploughs had been melted. They did it all over China. They did it where the soil was thin, and the topsoil blew away and the land has never recovered. They did it on the hillsides and destroyed the terraces that took generations to construct.'

'Why did they do that? Twelve feet deep!'

'Mao had some pet theorists, not real scientists, who promised to multiply the harvests. Mao thought that with enough belief, enough struggle by the people, whatever he wished would come true.'

'When you cut the earth so deeply, you are hurting the earth dragon,' Lumy said. 'That's what the farmers would believe. They would be afraid, that the dragon would be angry.'

'Yes. They'd know the new policies were an insult to the land, but they had to follow them. The other thing they had to do was close-sowing and close-planting. On the theory that it was good for plants to show mass strength and class solidarity, the seedlings were to be planted very thick and bunched together. Again, the peasants had to do what all their experience told them wouldn't work. How did that old man feel?' Peter asked softly. 'Forced to throw his precious seeds into those deep furrows, where they would never germinate. Forced to crowd the little shoots together so they couldn't grow. What violence was done to his integrity? Does he still remember the pain?'

* * *

On the sixth day, Lumy asked them whether they had any dirty clothes to be washed.

'Never mind lah,' said Alex. 'So cold here, we hardly sweat at all.'

'I'm waiting till we get to some hotel with a washing machine,' Katrina said. She had already, with great distaste, had to put on used garments. She hated the dust and dirt that seemed to be everywhere.

'I can't stand it! Must wash! I cannot stand to keep the clothes so dirty. I will get them washed,' Lumy said. She collected clothes from all of them. Katrina assumed that Lumy had found a washing machine, or perhaps a laundryman, in the village. The second time that Lumy collected their clothes, Katrina found her boiling a big pan of water to soak the laundry, then scrubbing and wringing by hand. Slightly appalled, Katrina went to help her.

Before they finished hanging the wet clothes out, Katrina's hands were aching with cold. She found herself pinning a pair of Alex's shorts on the line and laughed to herself. *Never thought I'd be doing laundry for that silly fellow!* she thought tolerantly.

* * *

The temperatures dropped. 'I'm damn cold,' said Peter, huddling on the brick platform.

Alex peered into the fireplace underneath. 'Can we get a better fire in here?' What the Changs used for fuel was dry corncobs and stalks, from the pile behind the house. The Singaporeans bought coal dust from the village shop and learned how to shape it into briquettes. The coal dust burned hotly, filling the room with acrid fumes but warming the brick platform well.

'Much warmer now,' said Alex. 'As long as we stay put on the bed. I'm really frightened of going out to the toilet!' Each night he made it his job to get up in the small hours, to keep the fire going.

'Are you okay, Peter?' Lumy asked.

Peter answered with distant regret. 'I'm running low on Percodan. And I may be getting pressure sores, from lying on my back all day.'

'Let's have a look,' said Lumy. Katrina, concerned, helped Lumy turn Peter on his side so that they could examine his back. Later, she noticed with surprise that she had not even remembered her usual revulsion in the face of injury and sickness.

There were red patches at the base of Peter's spine and at his hips. He explained that in hospital they'd rub the skin with alcohol, and use an air-ring to take the pressure off the affected areas. Katrina devised a support pad from a rolled tee-shirt. Alex bought a bottle of rice-spirits from the shop, and they took turns to rub Peter's back twice a day.

* * *

On the seventh day in Nanchiao, Katrina suggested that they should do another period of Listening, in the middle of the day. 'Since we have the time, we might as well put it to good use!' she suggested.

You're so scared to let even one minute be lost, huh? Bezalia mocked her gently. She sent Katrina pictures of her regular schedules at home: the intricate marquetry of appointments, the layered multi-tasking, so that if she only did one thing, walked or travelled or sat in the hairdressers', without simultaneously reading or writing or talking on the phone, she counted it as the waste of one time-slot, an opportunity lost.

After a while Katrina noticed that the aimlessness of the days no longer made her antsy. The three sessions of Listening began to colour all the day. In each period she again saw herself as precious, and the world as beautiful. After Listening, there was no other busy activity to erase that vision. She walked round the village, and from time to time she would feel that she could almost see the real face of things, that if she tried harder, she would see heaven shining out from the dirty street and shabby houses. Each dusty stone was a jewel. Each stolid peasant face was the face of a sleeping angel, unaware of inner divinity.

* * *

One evening, Lumy cooked them a special dish of fat pork and tofu and black soya sauce. Alex cracked some bottles of the local beer. After eating they sat around, replete, and contented. Peter was talking about the early days of the Spiritual Arts Centre.

Katrina looked at him and thought how much she had learned from Peter in the past weeks, just by watching his wisdom and patience. For a long time, she had wondered about his past life, and how he had been injured. Now she felt she knew him well enough to ask, though indirectly at first. 'Peter, how long have you known Bezalia? Have you always known her?'

Peter smiled at her, as though he knew what she wanted to ask. 'I've known her for fifteen years. It really began in 1983, when I was twenty-five years old, on top of the world in every way. A year later I was in a wheelchair, living on insurance money, and my fiancée had ditched me.' He told them the story.

* * *

Peter Fernandez wanted to reach the summit of the Himalayas and the top of the law profession, in that order. His plan for his life included ten years of active climbing before the age of thirty-five, while doing the obligatory drudgery in the lower echelons of Gomez Perchin Kamarrudin, and then a refocusing on career goals and a blitzkrieg charge for partnership, prominence, and lots of money. The two parts of the plan would complement each other. He would make all sorts of useful international contacts on the high trails and in the base-camps, and the public image of a mountaineer would later add to the charisma of a formidable courtroom personality.

As a mountaineer he had a good perception of his own strengths and weaknesses. He had good physical reflexes and sense of balance, his chief difficulty being to find enough exercise time during the working week. Mentally he had nerve and determination and was well aware that every climber needed to work as a member of the team.

The Singapore climbing team mounted an expedition to Annapurna, with Everest as an ultimate goal years down the line. They did three weeks of acclimatization. The accident happened on the third day out, at a low level, not even on the mountain proper.

Later, Peter would go repeatedly over the incident in his mind, asking himself what went wrong, what else should have been done. Hooked up to gleaming equipment in a hospital room, he would look back obsessively to the dim green forests and rushing white rivers of Nepal, with a load of anger and blame.

The team had made 1000 vertical metres that day, up one of the minor peaks and down again, carrying heavy packs. Peter was feeling lousy. He always had a bit of altitude-sickness for the first few days. Before leaving Singapore, he had been busy with a big CBT case, and had no time to get into condition.

Eric Lee, a less experienced climber, was ahead of Peter as they came down the last slope towards their camp. He was going too fast in the dim light. Peter should have pulled him back, told him 'The climb ain't over till you're off the mountain.' He didn't do so; he had a splitting headache and was in a hurry to get back to camp. Or perhaps he didn't want to look wimpish, with Jarek the expedition leader not far behind them; Peter was gunning for team leadership himself in the near future.

Eric came down to the little river near their camp. A line of stepping-stones crossed the river. Some distance below the crossing was a small waterfall, where the river plunged down twenty feet to stony rapids below.

Eric started jumping from one stone to the next, and whether in fatigue or carelessness, missed his step and fell into the river. It was swift but shallow. The current rolled him down the riverbed, yelling and cursing, and he ended up clinging to a rock ten yards from the waterfall.

The river was less than waist-deep. Peter scrambled down the riverbank and Jarek hurried after him. Peter came to level with Eric. 'Bloody fool!' he shouted cheerfully. 'Hang on there, I'll come and get you!'

'Get a rope!' Jarek shouted from up the riverbank. 'Peter, wait till we get a rope!' Peter pretended that he did not hear what Jarek shouted, in the noise of the rushing river. He felt Eric was his responsibility. He did not want Jarek taking over the rescue.

He waded out into the river, stretching his hand to Eric. Eric grabbed his hand. 'Don't let go!' Peter yelled, but Eric let go of the rock he was holding and clung with both hands to Peter. Peter lost his footing as Eric's weight came on him and the current pulled them both downstream. His head went under the surface, he spluttered in icy water.

'Look out! The waterfall!' Jarek shouted anxiously from the riverbank. Peter and Eric struggled together towards the bank. Jarek reached out and caught Eric's hand and pulled him to shore.

Peter was shivering with cold. He never quite knew how he slipped again on the stones. He fell back into the water and the current swept him over the little waterfall onto the rocks below.

Peter had few memories of the journey home. The expedition doctor shot him full of morphine, and Jarek organized an airlift from Pokhara. He came back to full consciousness in Mt Elizabeth Specialist Hospital, to find that he could not move his legs. Dr Chavathlu showed him X-rays and described the operations that had been done on his spine and pelvis. He would be a cripple for the rest of his life.

'I was bitter. I was mean,' Peter said, telling his story by dim firelight in Nanchiao. 'My fiancée stood by me, Rosalind, she tried to be supportive. I made all sorts of demands on her, and I made her life miserable.'

He went back home, with his shiny new wheelchair and a future of more operations and physiotherapy to look forward to. He felt he had a right for the whole world to be sorry for him.

He exploited Rosalind's sympathy. He manipulated her with pity and guilt.

He made her get into bed with him. He tried to drown his frustration in frequent and frenzied sex. He could get an erection, but he couldn't move: he could have sex but he had to be entirely passive. All his aggression had to be verbal. He would alternately beg and demand for Rosalind to meet his needs. 'But after I came, I would lie there and realize that I was so helpless and powerless. I couldn't really fuck like a man.'

He began asking Rosalind what she did each day and who she met. He questioned her about every movement throughout the day and quarrelled with her over her answers. One Sunday, she came to his house after Mass and told him with tears in her eyes that she was breaking off with him.

'She said that since my accident I had become totally selfish. I was trying to control her all the time. She couldn't stand it anymore, she had to go. I used every trick in the book to make her stay. I said I understood that she was leaving me because she didn't want to be tied to a cripple, but I really needed her. I said that I wanted to kill myself if she went away. She said that in that case, it was a good thing I couldn't get out of the chair to do it.'

After Rosalind left, Peter sank into deep depression. He refused to go for physiotherapy, would not let his mother and sisters put him into the chair in the mornings. He lay in bed 'wallowing in misery, feeling sorry for myself,' Peter related briskly, years later.

'Bezalia pulled me out of it. Late one night I thought someone came into my room. I knew I was awake because my back was aching like hell all the time; but it seemed like I was dreaming, because this woman just appeared and spoke to me. She was about thirty, wearing a little black dress that looked good on her. She said, *Peter, I know that you can't move your legs, you're paraplegic. I'm here to tell you that it doesn't really matter.*

'I said, *Don't give me that shit. I'm a cripple. I'm not a man anymore!* She smiled and she said, *In your mind, where it counts, you are still a man!* And then she proved it to me.'

In some strange place, Bezalia made love to Peter. In a way that was not physical, she welcomed him, and he went into her. Her love surrounded him, and he received her limitless self-giving. He felt enlarged, he felt more pride and self-confidence than he had ever found in courtrooms or on mountain tops. He reached a transcendent experience, something like a celestial orgasm that transformed earth and sky. He would never be the same again.

Peter finished telling his story. 'Bezalia lived with me ever after that,' he said. 'She taught me how to Listen and how to take a good hard look at myself. I began to see what a swine I had been. I got used to life in a wheelchair. Three years later, Rosalind married Joe Concencio and I sent them a nice present.'

Alex built up the fire and opened another bottle of beer. Wind blew round the house.

'I got to know you around that time,' Lumy said.

'Yes. You needed an office manager for the Spiritual Arts Centre. Bezalia told me to apply for the job.'

Alex asked what he had long wondered. 'Why is it called Spiritual Arts Centre?'

'All the activities there, in some way enrich the human spirit,' Peter explained. 'They help the spirit to grow—so that it becomes aware of the divinity within. You'd be surprised, how many people come into Listening, after they have been doing hapkido or clay-modelling for a while.'

Alex looked puzzled. 'How does hapkido link up to Listening?'

'You told me that you learned a bit of karate when you were in school. Weren't you taught about discipline and self-control?'

'Maybe that's why I dropped out!' Alex laughed.

'All the martial arts require you to be centred, to be focused and aware of yourself in the present moment. You learn clarity and mental discipline. The chaps who come to me from the hapkido class take to Listening like ducks to water.'

'I used to learn Japanese flower arrangement,' said Lumy. 'When you do this art, you can't be *luan,* you can't be all over the place. You have to be very centred, very still. When you arrange the flowers, you are aware of the whole universe. It helped me a lot, to be more focused, more concentrated. When I first met Bezalia, I was very scattered.'

Katrina looked at Lumy with a smile. She had learned to see the rock-like stability underneath Lumy's habitual garrulity and diffuseness of speech.

'It was twenty-five years ago,' said Lumy. 'I felt like I had nothing in my life, nothing to hold on to. I was married to Chan Leong, the children were in school. I spent a lot of time organizing social functions and dinners for charity. I depended on those activities to make my life feel important. Without them I felt very small! Like I was not a person at all!'

'I know what you mean,' Katrina said earnestly.

'Somehow I started going to Bezalia's Listening classes. Oh yes,' Lumy smiled and nodded proudly, 'I'm one of the few people who had that privilege, when Bezalia came and taught us in person! She had a house on a hill in Telok Blangah, it's gone now, they built a nice public park on the site. I went very regularly every week. I knew Bezalia was a wonderful teacher, someone very special. That was all I knew about her.'

* * *

Hot sunshine on the top of a hill; hot on the open lawn, and on the top of Lumy's head, as she made her way around the house, her high heels sinking into the neatly-shaven, broad-leaved grass, trickles of sweat running below her Ralph Lauren jacket, calling and calling: 'Bezalia!'

Smells of warm vegetation breathed from the grass and from overhanging trees. The house was silent. Its lower level was surrounded by deep verandas and porches. The tall doors leading onto the verandas were all closed. On the upper level a continuous row of windows ran around the house; they had no glass, but hinged window-leaves made of slatted wooden louvres always let in light and air. In the hot noonday all the window-leaves stood open, and a flock of eight sparrows flew from the branches of a tree into the house, and disappeared into its shadowy interior.

Lumy watched them enviously. Birds could enter Bezalia's house, but Lumy was locked out. Heat gathered behind her eyes and tension hardened in her throat. The pleasant half-smile on her face hardly changed. No tears broke through to smear the flawless surface of her powder and makeup, the carefully constructed facade of the successful society woman.

Maybe Bezalia was in the silent house, looking down from some shadowed window, hearing Lumy's calls but not replying, the way she never picked up her ringing phone, never returned the messages Lumy left for her. The only time Lumy could see her was at Thursday class.

Last Thursday, Lumy had tried to corner Bezalia, had broken the rules and interrupted the class, to buttonhole her teacher. Bezalia walked into the class and smiled at everyone and sat down. Everyone fell silent. And Lumy spoke up brightly: 'Bezalia! I want you to buy a ticket for my Spastic Children's Charity Dinner!'

'I don't go to dinners,' Bezalia replied mildly. The rest of the class shifted rebukingly. Lumy felt their disapproval like a weight pressing her down. It was a weight she had taught herself to disregard, whenever it might hinder what she needed to do. 'It's for *charity*,' she persisted, 'you will buy a ticket for a good cause, just come to the dinner!'

'No, Lumy, I'm not buying a ticket.'

Lumy hardly paused to breathe. 'Think of the poor little spastic children, Bezalia! Think what they have to suffer! You're so good-hearted, I know you'd want to do your bit to help them!'

'You don't know what I want,' Bezalia said softly. She looked at Lumy, and her eyes were fathomless, beyond Lumy's sounding. 'Lumy, don't try to manipulate me with false emotion. It doesn't work on me. It dishonours yourself.'

Lumy stopped with her mouth open, speechless. And Bezalia turned to the class and spoke the opening words of the session: 'Listen to stillness. Listen to silence. Listen to the voice of your heart.'

Lumy was not given to self-questioning. She did not ask herself why her failure to capture Bezalia's attendance at the dinner, was even more intolerable to her than other failure. She only knew discomfort, frustration, and a growing sense of futility, as she kept walking round Bezalia's house, calling and calling.

The surrounding trees seemed to swallow her voice. Heat and fatigue harassed her, she felt impotent, demeaned. 'Bezalia—' Her voice broke. She stood still. Unwilling to believe, she began to believe that she would not get what she wanted. She began to resign herself to leaving the hilltop with her purpose unfulfilled.

A brick path led down to the car park where Lumy's red Mercedes coupe was parked. Lumy started walking down the path. Behind her she felt the silent house looming, its many windows watching her walk away unsatisfied. Suddenly Lumy paused, standing still on the brick path that baked in the noonday heat; and a great sob burst out of her throat, shaking her body. A sense of deprivation or loss flooded her. She gasped and gasped again, in the grip of an emotion she did not understand.

Soon the dry sobs ceased. She opened her bag and carefully dabbed her eyes and checked her makeup, but her eyeliner was hardly smudged. She was glad that this had happened in a lonely place, with no one to see the elegant Mrs Lumy Chan in collapse. Again, she did not ask herself what was happening to her.

As she approached her car, she saw something white tucked under the windscreen wiper. With a driver's reflex anxiety, she looked about for a ticketing officer, even in this remote place. Closer, she saw it was an envelope, with her name written on it.

Inside the envelope was some money, and a slip of paper.

Lumy, please keep a ticket for me. I'll meet you at the dinner. Bezalia.

Lumy paused. 'I didn't realize then, how much I was asking of Bezalia. Now I know that it's hard for her to let people see her. When she used to come to teach us in person, she had to make a big effort, and I think when I disturbed the class like that, it was really painful to her.'

'But she accepted your invitation,' said Katrina.

'I think she came, in the end, because she knew that I wanted her more than I wanted anything else in the world. She heard my cry for help.'

* * *

Lumy stood at the entrance to the hotel ballroom, beneath heavy damask curtains on a thick crimson carpet, wearing her Cartier diamonds and Givenchy gown. From the ballroom came the clink of silver, the odour of good food. She met the high-society people who had bought tickets from her. She basked in their happy smiles, as they came in to the feast she had spread for them: the banquet of social approval and public esteem.

Bezalia came in. It seemed to Lumy as though the whole room looked different. The bright lights looked dimmer; the diamonds lost their sparkle. All the glitter of the room was subdued by the light that shone from Bezalia. Lumy cut short her pleasing remarks to the bank chairman and his wife who stood beside her and hurried to meet her valued guest. 'Bezalia! Thanks for coming! I'm so happy you could make it!'

She felt as proud as though the Queen of England were her guest. She turned to the dignitaries and introduced Bezalia proudly. 'Dato Wee, Datin, this is Bezalia, my meditation teacher!'

The chairman and his wife looked at Bezalia. They felt there was nothing remarkable about her, nothing important. They saw a woman in black, who made only a vague impression on their minds. They could register no details of her appearance, could not have said whether she was tall or short, old or young. They glanced at Lumy in some puzzlement and mumbled their greetings.

Lumy saw their eyes dismiss Bezalia as someone totally insignificant. In that instant she decided, not knowing how big the decision was, that if the people she admired couldn't see how wonderful Bezalia was, they were entirely wrong. She left the side of the tycoon and his wife, left her post of welcome. She took Bezalia's arm and walked her down the room to the place that had been reserved for her.

'Thank you for inviting me,' Bezalia murmured, smiling at Lumy. 'I'm glad I came.' The light around her seemed to glow around Lumy too. Lumy's arm tingled where she touched Bezalia. 'Thank you,' Bezalia said again, as Lumy installed her in her seat. She smiled into Lumy's eyes.

Lumy felt as though gold fire flowed in her veins. Her heart beat like music. She went back towards her guests of honour; and as she did, she felt as though she were eight feet high, as though she could pick up a table in one hand.

She saw her guests seated around their table. They all seemed beautiful, the old men venerable, the women queenly. Old Mr Wee was a kindly sage; every wrinkle in his face spoke of wisdom. He bowed to Lumy in respect and admiration. Isabella Wee glowed like the world's most elegant model, as she told Lumy how much she liked her dress. Lumy took Isabella's hand, she felt she was as elegant as Isabella, her equal in every way.

'Please eat,' she said to them. 'Enjoy the food.' Soon she had
to make a speech of thanks; and she felt all the people in the room
waited eagerly to hear her, treasuring her words. They applauded
in salute of who she was, Lumiere Chan, Bezalia's friend.

Once and for all, Lumy knew that her life was immensely
valuable, even if she never organized another charity dinner again.

* * *

As time went by, Lumy found that she no longer had the same
enthusiasm for her society work. She did not have to be busy all
the time. She began to decline requests to serve on committees.
Some years later, Bezalia said that she would no longer meet
students and conduct classes herself. She needed Lumy's help, to
make changes in the way Listening was brought to Singaporeans.

Lumy found a patron who leased them the house in Upper
East Coast Road and the Spiritual Arts Centre was established.
Masters of various art forms turned up, inquiring whether they
could hold classes there. Melissa and Peter taught Listening.

'We've been there for more than ten years now,' Lumy ended
her story. 'But really it is Bezalia's place. Bezalia is the one who
runs it.'

They sat and listened to the silence of the night.

Chapter Eighteen

Around the twelfth day—they no longer knew the count of days, without stopping to figure it out—Peter asked, 'Are you all still getting the flashbacks?'

Katrina grimaced. 'Even oftener now! Used to be two or three a day, now I had three already this morning.'

Alex growled, 'I had seven yesterday. Lucky I'm not in the office trying to work!'

Peter nodded. 'You too, Lumy? And me, depression, despair, frustration, hanging over my head all the time. It's like the projections are strongest here, in the middle of Henan, where the famine was worst.'

'This is where the hungry ghosts come from!' said Lumy.

Peter looked round his friends. 'We should make an effort to face them.'

Katrina laughed uncertainly. 'In Chinese movies, the hero battles the evil spirits with his magic kungfu!'

'Sorry man, I ain't no kungfu master! You know Bezalia always tells us that we have to face our inner demons. Are you willing to do that?'

'I am not afraid of demons,' Lumy said. 'We are safe because Bezalia looks after us. She won't let them hurt us.'

'What do we have to do?' Alex asked nervously.

'Nothing, except stop whatever you have been doing, to hold away the images. Look, you know you've been counting the flashbacks, trying to keep control. *Dammit, here they come again*, you say, and you resist. Just stop doing that!'

'I don't know how!' said Katrina.

'Make a decision now,' Peter said softly, 'to open up whatever gates you have kept closed. Let go of any barriers you have been holding. It is safe to do so. Allow in whatever has been trying to gain entry. Listen to whatever wants to speak to you. Listen to stillness. Listen to silence. Listen to the voices in your heart.'

Katrina listened. The images which had flashed past her like scenes glimpsed by lightning came flicking faster. They merged into a continuous scenario, of events observed from within. Her heart beat fast. *Bezalia, I'm scared. Like this horrible nightmare stuff is going to swallow me up!*

I will be with you all the time. You will not be harmed.

She was looking at something grey. A grey spot which was a patch of ashes on a cold hearth. Ashes where a cooking fire had been; a fire that had gone out, fourteen months ago.

Katrina felt a small burden in her arms. Across her vision moved a pale thing shaped like a star. It was a tiny hand, coming from the bundle she carried. A small voice wailed. That little hand did not look the way a baby's hand should look. It was a greyish-blue colour. It was fleshless, without chubby padding of wrist and palm. It came groping at the faded blue cotton of the mother's coat, and the cry rose, hoarse and weak.

The woman whose life Katrina shared, looked dully at her son. Her heart was a dry riverbed, cracked clay at the bottom of an empty reservoir. Slowly her hand went to the buttons of her coat. Her hand was very thin, dirty, and rough, lined with bleeding cracks. She laid bare her breast, that was only a loose pouch of skin, and put the brown nipple to the infant's lips. He grabbed eagerly with his mouth. She winced with the pain but let the baby suck and chew. No milk flowed for him. She could not feed her son.

Oh my god, said Katrina, her heart aching, wanting to cry, while at the same time she felt the woman's dull despair. *This is awful, Bezalia! It's too much!*

I am here with you. Katrina, watching from within the starving woman in horror and pity, felt Bezalia watching too.

The walls of the hut were mud bricks. There were gaps in the bricks for door and windows, and in the openings were propped screens of woven canes which darkened the house but did not keep out the cold. Dust stirred around the woman's feet as wind blew through the gaps.

Steps outside. Someone stopped and called for entrance. The woman felt a wave of fear, as a man in a green uniform entered the hut. 'You peasants are hiding food!' he shouted.

The woman kept her head down and looked at the floor. From the corners of her eyes she watched the soldier as he prodded the crevices of the deserted kitchen with an iron rod. He kept on shouting. 'The harvests have been good. There is plenty of grain. You are hiding it, you traitors, you criminals!' He prodded the earth floor of the house.

The woman's heart beat fast as the soldier approached the far side of the room, where there was a patch of new mud in the wall. Katrina saw her memory of two days ago.

She stood in a line of people holding chopsticks and eating bowls, at a communal kitchen. Nowhere else were they allowed to cook and eat. Cooks brought in big tubs. The tubs were filled with thin watery gruel, mixed with leaves and tree bark. The people pushed and struggled for the food. The woman got only a few drops in her bowl.

She carried her child into the fields far from the village. She gathered grass and lit a small fire. In a tin cup she boiled water and cooked a half-handful of grain that she had saved. She made a soft mash and pushed it between the baby's pale lips. She returned and hid the remainder of the grain in the wall of the house.

Katrina knew the woman trembled as the soldier searched the house. *I'm scared, Bezalia! Something terrible is going to happen!*

Yes, said Bezalia. Katrina saw that in the sky above the hut hovered the storm-dragon. On its brow rode the Lady of the Winds, looking down with a face of stern compassion.

The man who searched the house drove his iron rod into the wall, and the new mud fell in fragments. With them fell a tin cup and a small package wrapped in cloth. He seized the package and scattered the grain on the floor. 'You were hiding food!'

The soldier swung the iron rod to the woman's head. Half-stunned she dropped her son. The baby wailed. She fell to the floor scrabbling to pick him up. The iron rod came down on the baby's head with a cracking sound, and his cries stopped.

The woman screamed and writhed on the floor. Her agony was a storm which filled Katrina's mind.

Through the tempest came the storm-dragon, its eyes blazing bright, with Bezalia riding on its brow. Strong and slender, her robes streaming in the gale, she dropped down from the sky. Light came from her and lit the darkness, as the dragon hovered low over the room.

The iron rod crashed onto the woman's head. In the moment she died, Bezalia swooped down, reaching out to catch the woman in her arms. The dragon roared and surged upward through the clouds. The woman and her child stood with Bezalia, mounted on the dragon, rising with her away from the earth, out of Katrina's sight.

Katrina opened her eyes, seeing her friends sitting anxiously beside her. 'Are you all right? You were sobbing and crying!' said Alex.

They saw Katrina sigh deeply, and rub her hands over her face. All around them there was a sense of peace, like the clear air after a storm.

'She's gone. The one who was suffering—Bezalia took her away.' The woman's presence was gone from Katrina's mind, with its anguish and despair. She thought she would experience no more flashbacks.

* * *

A day or two later it was Alex's turn to freak out. A few Listening periods had gone by peacefully and Alex had begun to hope he wouldn't have any alarming experiences. In the middle of a session the others heard him groaning and calling out. He fell backward and thrashed around; they heard the thump of his head on the bricks of the platform, and his flying fist caught Lumy full in the mouth. She pushed a folded blanket under his head. He lay shuddering and jerking and shouting incoherently.

He saw himself wearing a crisp uniform, standing in front of a crowd of people. He had a revolver in his belt, a drawn knife in his hand. The people wore shabby clothes. Their eyes burned in thin faces. Alex, staring back, saw his brother Chuan among them, and Choo the supplier, and Elder Lim from the church: all haggard and dressed in rags.

'You are all criminals!' he heard himself cry out. 'I have to kill you!' Alex felt as though the words were being torn from his own aching throat. He felt the anguish of the man holding the knife, his rage at the people and at himself. At the same time, he was conscious of his own body flailing about on the bricks. He was able to watch the scenario in his mind with a kind of detachment, with the awareness of Bezalia watching with him.

He pushed into the crowd and grasped a woman like his mother by her greasy grey hair. His heart pounded and leaped in his chest. 'Open your mouth!' he cried. She shook her head and clenched her teeth. He set the knife between her lips and pressed her mouth open, the blade grating harshly on her teeth. White grains spilled from the old grey lips, mixed with her blood.

Alex struggled on the brick platform and gasped for breath. He was appalled by what he was seeing. *Why are you doing this?* he shouted in his mind.

I was afraid! the man whose nightmare Alex was sharing called back to him. *I had to punish them, or I would suffer! I was afraid!*

What a horrible thing you did! Alex said.

I had to do it! the man cried to Alex.

Alex shared the man's memories. He saw a climate of terror. Of arbitrary accusations and hysterical hate. People whom he had always known were designated as enemies. Afraid for his own life, he saw hangings, shootings, deaths by hot irons and by ingenious torture.

He was standing among other soldiers. He was dragged out from the ranks and accusations were thrown at him like stones. He was yelled at and condemned. He was forced to kneel, arms outstretched behind him, for excruciating hours.

He had been one of the righteous and powerful, suddenly he was worthless, reduced to nothing. He wanted to say whatever they wanted, so that he could be restored to his place. He wanted to hate the enemies of the people.

He became part of the machine of terror, and also its victim.

Pity him, Alex heard Bezalia's voice.

What terrible things he did, said Alex.

He was powerless, said Bezalia. *Nothing in his life gave him strength to stand against the flood.*

In the nightmare he shared with Alex, the soldier faced the crowd of ragged people, and the one who looked like Chuan. He felt tears streaming down his face and running salt into his mouth. He lunged forward with his knife and slit open Chuan's belly. The purple liver spilled out, the other organs red and green. Among them showed a quantity of white grains. The man dropped the knife and with his hands scooped up the warm steaming mass of grain.

The pain in his heart spread down his body. He looked down and saw that his own belly had been opened. His viscera fell out;

the coils of gleaming intestine slipped out wetly with an awful feeling of emptying. His heart still beat, between the lungs, above the hollow cavity of his belly: knowing emptiness, hollowness, the pain of betrayal.

Help me! Alex saw the soldier standing in front of him, face to face, the lower part of his body bloody and hollow. He stretched out his bloodstained hands to Alex. *Help me!*

I don't know what you want! Alex cried. The man's eyes glared at Alex; his mouth moved. His hands gestured in desperate need. *I don't know how to help you!* Alex said.

He heard Bezalia's voice. *Only you can help him. You can forgive him.*

Alex took a step towards the man, gazing into his face, seeing his pain. *I understand,* Alex said to him.

The man was weeping. He sobbed and moaned. He looked at Alex with tears running down his face and stretched out his hands beseechingly.

Alex went closer and reached out. *I forgive you*, he said, and took the hands of the other man in his own.

His hands were grasped and held tightly. He heard the other man gasp and cry with relief as they made a connection, a bridge between two humans. And he felt Bezalia leap across that bridge, as power surges through a cable link into a distant network. The other man cried out again, in love and gratitude and surprise.

The other man faded from Alex's consciousness: and the blackness which carried him away, was the blackness of Bezalia's robe.

Alex opened his eyes calmly on the sleeping-platform and asked for a drink of water.

Chapter Nineteen

Each day seemed long, but the days flowed by unnoticed. In the frosty weather, they went outside less, spent more time sitting together. Sometimes hardly a word was spoken, between one Listening session and the next.

'How are you, Lumy?' Peter asked over dinner one night. 'Are you still picking up those disturbing emotions?'

'Not so bad now,' Lumy replied. 'It improved a lot, since I started cooking regularly.' Every night now she cooked their meal, improvising with local spices and condiments. Katrina helped her, setting herself to learn new skills. The Changs watched with immense interest, and Lumy gave them portions of each dish.

'You know I used to feel how those hungry people suffered,' Lumy said. 'The other day when I was preparing food, I felt them all around me. Starving people, saying to me, *You can eat well, but we had to starve!* I spoke to them in my heart. *Come and eat,* I said to them. *I want to welcome you to eat with us.* All the time I was cooking, I was talking to those people, asking them to share in our meal. *Take it. Eat,* I was inviting them. I felt their painful complaining get less. I do this every time I cook now. I feel as though they are more contented.'

'So, you're feeding the hungry ghosts,' smiled Peter.

'I don't understand,' said Alex. 'When we get to Chengshen, are we going to make offerings to the dead in the traditional way? Are we going to offer food and burn paper money? That is like pagan superstition you know!'

'No,' said Peter. 'We don't need elaborate symbols of respect to the dead.'

'People spend a lot of money on those paper models!' Alex said heatedly. 'I've seen fully-furnished paper houses all ready to be burned up, complete with TV and VCR and all the luxury goods. And a life-size Mercedes car!'

'Modern style these days,' Katrina said with cheerful scepticism, 'instead of burning lots of paper money, you can just burn a replica credit card!'

'Yes, well, some people take the traditional symbols too literally,' Peter agreed. 'We will hold a very simple ceremony at Chengshen.'

'What about you Peter, how are you doing with the bad vibes?' Katrina asked.

Peter sighed deeply. 'I still hear voices calling: *Feed us.* It's wearing me down, like a nagging headache, a constant feeling of frustration and despair. But it's not only food they want, I understand that now. This is the cry of people who lack basic needs to feed their souls. This is the spiritual hunger of those who died thirty years ago, and those who have lived through the years since then.

'I have felt this ever since we got to China. Remember the people at the Dongshandu airport? They acted as though they could not see us, could not hear us, as people like themselves. I have a sense of people who have become isolated from each other, and from their own inner truth. The policies of China in the past three decades have been designed, it seems, to break down the connections that linked people to each other: and to their past, and to their land.'

Peter looked up suddenly and laughed. 'Bezalia tells me, It's not quite that bad, Peter! The human spirit is incredibly resilient. We can see that the people in this village haven't been destroyed, they have survived. But I think they have been wounded, in their capacity to love and trust. This was the centre of the famine, remember? But no one talks about it. No one admits that the government inflicted it upon them. No one remembers the dead.'

'How are we going to deal with that hunger, Peter?' Katrina asked.

'I don't know,' Peter replied calmly. 'I'm not in charge of this expedition, I've been clearly informed of that! We just have to carry out our instructions: find the field in Chengshen, and light candles there. The rest is not up to us.'

* * *

Lumy, Alex, and Katrina began to get worried about Peter. 'My feet feel numb,' he told them one day. 'The circulation in my legs is bad. I need you to manipulate the legs and rub my feet.'

Alex tried it first. Katrina watched him rather anxiously, wondering whether she would be able to perform correctly when it was her turn. Mrs Chang came in and watched with great interest.

'We are helping him to exercise,' Alex explained. She nodded in understanding, massage and exercise were familiar procedures to her. The other Changs passed by and told Peter's friends that they were doing the right thing for him.

Peter lay at the centre of this interest. *Funny, Bezalia, it should be embarrassing, humiliating—yet I hardly mind at all. My friends are devoting so much time and effort to me. I am so grateful to them.*

Your friends are happy, to find a focus for these inactive days. Peter, you are helping your friends more than you know. You have given them the opportunity, to reach out with hands of love.

A wide sore appeared on Peter's back. It grew wider and deeper day after day. 'Try to keep it from getting infected,' Peter said. The village shop had few medical supplies, no antibiotics. They did their best to keep the wound clean, changing the dressings often. The Changs' *Laopoh*, the old grandmother, let them use the kitchen steamer to sterilize the bandages. The Changs looked at the wound and shook their heads as it continued to deteriorate.

'I finally figured it out,' Alex said one day, 'the Changs think we all belong to the one family! I've been hearing them say *Your mother, your wife*—they think that Lumy is our mother, I'm the number-one son. Katrina is the daughter-in-law, and Peter and me must be brothers! Maybe they think Singaporeans are so strange anyway, can have Indian brothers.'

They are ignorant about ethnic differences, came Bezalia's voice. *They recognize love: such love as they believe can only exist between members of one family.*

* * *

One day, the Sixth Aunt went up to Katrina. She was a woman of about fifty, who seldom spoke to anyone. 'You should use sesame oil,' she said to Katrina. Her face hardly moved as she spoke. 'Sesame oil to dress the wound.'

They found a bottle of sesame oil—a luxury food item—in the village store. They used bandages soaked in sesame oil as a soothing, antiseptic dressing for Peter's wound. 'Feels good,' Peter said. These days he had little strength for talking.

When the Sixth Aunt saw them using it, she almost smiled. 'Sesame oil is good to use, it's really helpful,' Katrina said to her. She felt a spark of response in the other woman. She went on, trying to chat as Lumy would have done. 'You were so kind to give us that advice. We did not know about it, but since you advised us, we tried using the sesame oil. It is very good!'

'Sesame oil is very good!' said the woman.

'My name is Katy,' Katrina said, giving the Chinese equivalent of her name.

A smile. 'I am called Pei Yi.'

* * *

Katrina, rubbing Peter's limbs one day, felt Bezalia very close to them. They had finished their afternoon Listening and without speaking a word, Alex and Katrina took their places on either side of Peter, while Lumy went to the kitchen to hover over the cooking-fire.

Katrina rolled up Peter's left trouser leg. His skin was dry, wrinkled, discoloured with small broken veins: a sight whose ugliness did not occur to Katrina at all, as she put some lotion on her palms and began gently rubbing it in. She worked up the thin leg to the thigh, then returned to his foot to rub and manipulate it. She did the work unhurriedly. There was all the time in the world, for a task that was to be done each day.

Her hands moved slowly on Peter's body: and she felt as though she was caring for herself. She felt a powerful current flowing through her hands, of love and compassion for the flesh she worked on. It flowed into Peter, and back again into herself. It flowed from Alex too, as he worked on the other side of Peter, from Alex through Peter's body, to Katrina, and back to Alex. A dynamic rhythm of love given and received, a joyful current binding them together. She could hear Lumy's voice in the kitchen, and it seemed as though she too was part of their one body.

Katrina looked up, with her eyes full of tears. Alex smiled back at her. She saw Peter watching them peacefully.

There was no need for words. She just kept on working in silence, listening to the harmony around them.

* * *

Lumy knew both how to be busy and how to be still. The others saw her, outside the times of meditation, constantly doing chores in the kitchen and in the living space. While she cut vegetables and folded clothes, her mind was attentive to silence, to Bezalia's presence within her.

She looked up from her work one day and saw the Sixth Aunt, Pei Yi, sitting nearby. She seemed to be busy cleaning vegetables, but Lumy seemed to be hearing some unspoken message.

Lumy began to chat in her mixture of tongues. She could understand the local speech now. She got Pei Yi to talk to her; learned that she was the widow of the sixth son of the Chang family who had died ten years ago. She had two sons which gave her status in the family.

Help me out Bezalia, I have to find out what's troubling this poor girl. Lumy said casually, 'You know we want to go Chengshen! Do you know what kind of a place it is?'

'I know Chengshen.'

'Oh! If you know the place, please tell me about it! You can help us!'

'I was born in Chengshen.'

'You were born there?' repeated Lumy. She felt a pang of sorrow. She looked into Pei Yi's face, reached out and took her hands. 'When did you leave Chengshen?' she said softly.

Pei Yi's eyes filled with tears. 'I left when I was ten years old,' she said. Lumy stared at her in shocked surprise. Pei Yi began to speak steadily, the words pouring out of her without break. 'My mother died of hunger. My little brother died. Many people died. I remember them.'

Tears rolled down Lumy's cheeks as she listened. She mopped her eyes and blew her nose repeatedly, as she listened to the story of the child who was sent away from her home.

* * *

Pei Yi spoke of the village where for two years they had not had enough food. They ate grass and insects and the bark of trees. She shivered in winter cold in a thin rag, for they had eaten the cotton stuffing of their coats. Her older brother lay in the house. His body was swollen with water. His skin was full of ulcered sores.

Pei Yi was too weak to walk. She crawled on hands and knees along the path behind their house, going to the fields to search for ants and caterpillars. She paused often to struggle for breath and let her pounding heart subside.

She passed behind the house of her father's cousins—everyone in the village was related—and heard them speaking inside. They said that one of their aunts had killed her own daughter for food, had secretly cooked her flesh and eaten it. Pei Yi went home in fear. She saw her father sitting beside her dying brother. He stared at Pei Yi. She fell on her knees and begged her father, 'Don't eat me! Please don't eat me!'

Her father said that he would never eat his child, but he intended to sell her to a family in the nearest town. The people who bought Pei Yi would give her food, and the money would save her family.

Pei Yi had no complaints about the way she had been treated, by her father or by the family who bought her. She worked hard and found a good husband. She never heard from her father or brother again.

'I heard that everyone there died in the famine,' she told Lumy.

'Everyone!' Lumy repeated. 'Did you ever see their graves?'

'I have never gone back to Chengshen. When my grandmother died in the first year of the famine, she was properly buried, but later there were no funerals. My uncle fell down in the street and my aunt was already dead, there was no one to take him away. His body lay there for a long time. There were dozens of bodies lying in the street, they did not decay because there was no flesh on them to rot. Later they were taken to a field outside the village. They were piled up in a heap, and the snow fell and covered them.'

'That is terrible,' sighed Lumy. 'Maybe that field is the one we are looking for. Could you tell us how to find it?'

'Yes. There was a river, there was a big tree. I remember that field. I remember everything.'

Lumy told her friends about the pitiful story she had heard. 'She lived through the famine. She remembers it, it's still so painful in her memory! And I think she knows the place we want to go. I have asked her to come tonight, to tell us how to find the field in Chengshen.'

Pei Yi came in to the store room in the evening, when Lumy was rubbing Peter's feet; and while she repeated her story, she sat down beside Lumy and started working on Peter too. Next morning, she came again bringing a bottle of strong-smelling oil and spent an hour massaging Peter's legs with it. Her visits became part of their routine; her brusque friendship, part of their lives in Nanchiao.

Chapter Twenty

'I'm so sick of this steamed bread!' Alex complained at breakfast one day. 'So pale and damp, sticks to my teeth but it doesn't fill me up!'

Peter spoke quietly. 'In the times of food shortage, the government advised the people to double-steam the buns—steam them twice so that they'd swell up and be more filling. Another lie, another appearance without real substance.'

'I used to bake bread in Los Angeles,' said Lumy. 'There is an oven in the kitchen here. I'll try it out!' Over several days she experimented with the wood-fired oven and the local flour and yeast. The fragrance of baking filled the house. Her friends applauded her efforts and eagerly ate up even the less successful results. One evening, she produced a brown crusty loaf which all agreed was splendid. The Chang family each tasted a little piece with much appreciation.

'I will bake more tomorrow,' Lumy said. 'You must help me, Alex, because it takes a lot of strength to do the kneading! I'll make a big batch of bread, and some other dishes, and we can invite the Changs to join us for a meal!'

Preparations for the feast began. Alex rolled up his sleeves to knead the bread. 'Hey, when I go back, I can open a bakery!' he said, arms white to the elbow, pummelling and slapping the big bolster of dough on the floured board. Katrina, wincing and squealing, helped to kill, pluck and gut four chickens.

In the middle of this activity, they heard the rumble of a distant vehicle, on the road which had so long been silent. A string of vehicles came down the road from Chengshen. The people came out of their houses. Alex ran outside with his floury hands. 'The road is open! We can travel again!'

The friends Alex had made in the village crowded around him. 'The road is open! You can go to Chengshen!' they assured him with beaming faces. People reached out and slapped him on the back. 'Tomorrow the bus will come, you can make your journey,' they said happily. The village hummed with excitement.

There were a lot of people in the eating-shop as mealtime approached. The house was full of the fragrance of new-baked bread. Lumy made hurried arrangements with the Chang family. Alex spoke to the villagers: 'Please join us for a meal!'

They ate together in a festival atmosphere. Peter and his wheelchair were now a familiar sight. The villagers' friendly interest was directed to the bowls of food, and the big loaves with crisp brown crust.

Lumy stood laughing and talking, calling people by name and joking with them, while she sliced bread with a long knife. 'Please take bread!' she cried. 'Don't be shy! Please eat!' It did not seem there would be enough for all, but somehow the slices of bread kept coming and everyone had some.

The local school teacher and the party officer sat together. Alex made a point of talking to them and thanking them for the village's hospitality.

'So, if the bus comes tomorrow, you will be leaving us!'

'Yes, we will be going on to Chengshen at last. It is not much further on, is it?'

'Two or three hours,' mumbled the teacher, as though he didn't want to admit even that much knowledge of Chengshen. But Pei Yi stopped beside them, with a basket of bread that she was helping to pass around.

'To ride the bus to Chengshen is quite easy,' she said. 'I am going to come with you!'

'Oh, that's excellent!' Alex said, in surprise and pleasure. 'Yes—you come with us and help us find the place!'

'Oh, you're going, are you?' muttered the political officer, with a frown of disapproval.

'When I was young, I came from Chengshen!' Pei Yi said loudly. 'Now I am going back again!' And she went on happily serving the bread.

After a while, Peter asked Katrina to take him inside and help him out of the chair. He lay on the brick platform, listening to the party still going on. He hurt all over. The cold made him ache in interesting new places, added to the familiar deep ache of the old fractures, and the bite of the bedsore on his butt. He had run out of painkillers long ago. Sitting up in the chair for a few hours had been an ordeal. He wondered how he would make the journey to Chengshen.

Looks like we're going to get to Chengshen at last, Bezalia. What are we going to do there?

You are going to perform the ceremony you've prepared.

But what will we achieve by performing it?

Achieve, Peter? You will recognize the deaths of the thirty million, that is all you set out to do.

Yeah, okay. For that we've spent all this time in this little village, this wide place in the road in the middle of nowhere?

One thing you achieved in Nanchiao, is that Pei Yi rediscovered her lost past. Be pleased about that!

Yes, that's good. It's nice the way she's become so friendly with us, bosses us around like an old aunty . . .

Peter opened his eyes to find Pei Yi standing by him with a steaming bowl of liquid. She urged him to drink it. He sat up with difficulty and drank the bitter brew.

Katrina came in and found him handing the empty bowl back to Pei Yi. 'How can you just drink that stuff; you don't know what the hell it might be!'

'I presume it is some traditional medicine, I don't suppose it will hurt me. Frankly right now I'm prepared to try anything.'

'She says it will help the pain.'

Peter hardly heard. There was a ringing in his ears and the world seemed to be dropping away beneath him. He seemed to be rising through infinite darkness. The dark was lit by connected traceries of light, branching constellations in the huge sky.

Are you there Bezalia? He thought disjointedly, *I think I'm flying . . .*

Always with you, Peter.

He still felt pain, not localized in his distant body but everywhere, spread throughout the universe. The earth's pale globe lay far below him, white as the moon. From it rose moaning and weeping, sighs, and cries of pain. He heard the cries of the starving, and the ones who died by violence and brutality, and those still living in despair.

Bezalia!

I am here. Bezalia spoke close to him, holding him against her breast.

The sorrow and agony of multitudes entered Peter and mixed with his own anguish. He no longer knew whether the grief in him was his own or the others'. He felt the need and anger of all the troubled, mixing with all the anger of his own life and his knowledge of pain and frustration.

His heart ached as though it would burst and kill him. He was choking under a suffocating pressure. He was racked with pain, paralysed with sorrow.

Come lower, said Bezalia.

He seemed to be descending towards the earth. There was China below him, and Singapore away over the curve of the horizon. Dark clouds of misery hung above the plains. He saw again the endless crowd, calling out their need. Skeletal ragged figures, and to his surprise there were Singaporeans among them, people whom he knew, looking pale and unhappy and stretching out their hands. Their pain and deprivation ached in his heart. Their cry rang in his ears.

Oh my god, Bezalia, I can't stand much more of this.

All right. It's okay. Hang in there.

He saw the village of Nanchiao. He seemed to be looking down on the platform where his body lay, with his friends around him. Lumy and Pei Yi were there. Alex and Katrina were on each side of him, working on his feet. He felt full of gratitude for their devoted care.

He could feel the gentle pressure of their hands. They were rubbing and stretching his feet. Pei Yi knelt above him, kneading his body.

I am bread to be broken, Peter thought, not knowing where the thought came from.

He saw a bright aura of light around them. It streamed out of their hands and glowed through his passive body. It shone in a bright aura around them. Their work was generating energy from his carcase.

Bread to feed the hunger of the world.

A power bigger than any of them was mounting, building potential like lightning stored in massive thunderheads.

He saw Bezalia in the room, standing tall and slender at his head. She leaned down and scooped up energy from the group. She stood up and she was taller than the hills, her head touching the sky, her hands filled with power.

All round her came the wailing of the multitude: a tempest blowing across the world, the endless cry of those who suffer. Bezalia raised both hands high. Lightning arced between her fingers. Her voice rose high, piercing the storm.

Be fed!

Thunder bammed across the sky as Bezalia flung the lightning. It lit up the world. Where it fell, the mourning crowds had disappeared. Again and again she threw, in huge armfuls of showering energy. Rain began to fall. Torrents of rain, flooding the stony plain, filling dry reservoirs and riverbeds. Thunder rolled.

Relaxing, relieved of pain and tension, Peter's consciousness sank towards darkness and sleep. As he fell, he saw green spreading over the plain. The flooded fields were full of growing grain; and below the surface of the water lay a vast face smiling at the sky.

* * *

Next morning, the Singaporeans sat in the eating shop with their bags ready and packed, wondering whether the bus would come any time that day or the next. Pei Yi sat with them, with a flask full of her medicinal brew for Peter. Pick-up trucks and motorbikes passed along the road, stirring up clouds of dust. After the days of quiet, the sense of movement was exhilarating. They felt as though they were going to escape from confinement: 'Like the army boys on ROD!' Alex said.

'Look! Is that the bus coming?' Katrina cried.

The bus rattled down the road and drew up in front of the eating-shop. 'The bus is here!' the villagers cried, rushing to help the travellers on board. Pei Yi got onto the bus with them. The bags and the wheelchair were lifted to the roof.

At the front of the bus sat three men in metropolitan clothes, loaded with camera equipment. 'Hello, Peter Fernandez!' said one of them. Astonished, they recognized Tony Li.

'What on earth are you doing here!' Peter exclaimed.

'We're going to do a shoot at Chengshen!' Tony Li replied. As the bus pulled out of Nanchiao, the Singaporeans talked eagerly to Tony Li, and they never looked back.

Tony Li explained that after meeting them at the airport, he had begun to work on a great new project. 'I said, I must make the film. I must tell this story that no one knows about, it will be sublime! I interviewed a man in LA who lived in China in the 1960's. He remembered everything! I talked to Westinghouse and Lucasvision, I put the package together. I thought that I'll go to Chengshen and shoot those graves you were talking about. Did you find them? Have you gone there yet?'

'We were stuck in that village for weeks; the road was blocked! Didn't they tell you about it in Zhengzhou?'

'Nope, never heard about that,' said Tony Li.

He introduced his assistants, Johnny the cameraman and Foo with the sound recorder, cheerful young Hong Kongers who proffered cigarettes and cans of beer.

'Have you found out where the graves are?' Tony Li asked again.

'We aren't quite sure,' said Alex, 'but that lady, Chang Pei Yi, used to live in Chengshen forty years ago.'

Tony Li nodded purposefully. He gathered up cigarettes and notebook and moved across the bus to talk to Pei Yi, as the bus rattled on through Henan county.

In the early afternoon the bus entered a town of new brick buildings. There was a building whose sign read 'Chengshen Bicycle Factory,' and a street of shops. The bus stopped outside a small hotel, where the travellers found rooms and a restaurant with karaoke.

The Singaporeans would have liked to rest in the hotel rooms, but Tony Li had no time to waste. An hour later, they found themselves climbing into a small van he had rented somewhere. There was room in the van for the technicians and their equipment, as well as the wheelchair and all the people. Tony Li got behind the wheel and drove through the town. It seemed almost entirely new. 'Looks like they totally rebuilt the place, after all the people died!'

Pei Yi sat next to Tony Li. She pointed here and there. 'The school was there. The medicine shop was there.' They could not see what landmarks she might be going by.

'Are you sure?' asked Alex.

'I remember,' Pei Yi said, pressing her lips together. 'I remember everything.'

They halted outside another big building. 'Chengshen Piping Factory' said the sign.

'There is the field,' Pei Yi said. She pointed to the back yard of the factory. It was surrounded by a few strands of barbed wire. A lot of bicycles were parked on the cemented area, and some rusting abandoned machinery, among patches of mud and snow.

'This is it?' Tony Li said doubtfully.

'Yes. There is the river, there is the tree.' A big tree grew at the edge of the cemented area, next to a small dirty stream. 'This is the field where they left the bodies.'

They stood at the edge of the expanse of cement, near what seemed to be the back gate of the factory building. Tony Li looked around with measuring eyes.

'Okay. We'll set up the table over there, under the big tree.' While the Singaporeans hesitated, Tony Li and his assistants propped up the strands of barbed wire and ducked through the fence. They carried their equipment across the icy parking lot, while Alex and Katrina unloaded two large bags they had brought from Singapore.

'I'll do the interview with you first,' Tony Li said to Peter. 'Just an establishing shot under the tree, we'll go into the studio some other time.' He got the wheelchair positioned to his liking in the pale winter sunlight. He talked to Peter with his assistants filming them, their breath steaming in the gathering cold. He asked Peter why he had come to Chengshen.

Peter spoke as simply as he could, as Tony had earlier told him to do. He was just a passive observer now, other people had the enterprise in hand. He felt a slight sense of unreality as he answered the questions, heightened by a small dose of Pei Yi's painkiller that he had swallowed.

Someone approached across the expanse of cement. 'Here they are, coming to ask what we are doing here!' said Tony Li. He met the officer with an outstretched microphone and a flood of explanations. The camera focused on the man's face as Tony Li told him that they wished to pay respect at the graves of people who perished in the famine of 1959–62. The officer objected and floundered and soon retreated back to the factory.

'I caught the expression on his face!' said Tony Li. 'He knew what happened in this field!'

'If the authorities don't like what you're doing, they may confiscate your cameras and film,' Peter said.

'No film!' Tony Li said with a grin. 'I'm sending the pictures direct to LA on the satellite phone link. It's already being recorded at the studio.'

Meanwhile Alex, Katrina and Lumy made their preparations. They had borrowed a folding table from the hotel. They covered it with a white cloth and set out candles and cups.

The factory gates opened. Two men came out and strode towards the party, while behind them workers poured out of the factory. Some made for their bicycles and rode away; most came to watch their superiors confronting Tony Li.

Surrounded by a crowd, Tony Li asked the officers what they thought about the famine that had killed so many. Flustered, they dodged the questions and said they would not permit the visitors to hold their ceremony on the factory premises.

Tony Li reminded them that the wise national leadership had stated the freedom of religious observance. He had come to record this admirable development, with an international observer in tow—he pointed to Peter. He would be proud to introduce on television these local administrators who carried out national policy. Flattered, hypnotized by the camera, they smiled into the lens for him.

'Are you ready?' Tony Li called to the Singaporeans, as the winter afternoon was fading. The table had been set with white

candles and silk flowers. There was a jar of incense sticks and a
row of wineglasses.

They began the simple ceremony that Peter had devised. Each
person in turn offered wine and incense to unseen presences
around them. Alex, whose church forbade it, and Peter, who had
no ancestors in this country, made the offering. Silently each held
up a burning stick of incense and placed it in the jar. They lifted
up a glass of wine and poured it out on the earth. Lumy and
Katrina did the same.

Pei Yi followed Katrina. She held up a cup of wine and
raised her head, and she called out, 'Old ancestors, I'm here to
honour you!' To their amazement she began to chant and mourn
aloud. 'My mother and my father, you have died and gone away.
I don't see you anymore. I have come to honour you, my parents.
I remember you were virtuous and good. You died in famine, you
had no food to eat. You suffered and were lost. I do not forget
you, I remember.'

The watching people stood very still. No one moved or
breathed. Pei Yi placed one incense stick in the jar and took
another and continued her lament. 'My uncle, my aunt, you died
of hunger. There was no rice in your bowls, you grew thin and
weak. Why did you die? They took away your harvest, they broke
into your stores. You were killed by enemies of the people. I will
never forget.'

The woman's hoarse voice echoed across the expanse of
concrete. More incense sticks, more names, naming the dead of a
lost village. *How can she remember them all?* Katrina wondered. *When
did she learn to chant like this? And how does she dare?* The crowd stood
watching. Many of them must remember the famine too.

The young cameraman had tears running down his cheeks
that he could not wipe away, as he kept his lens pointed at Pei Yi.
The stream of images went into the networks, flashed across the
world to distant studios. The lament vibrated across the world.

Pei Yi's long chant ended, and she stepped back. Tony Li signalled to Johnny to stop filming. He went forward and made the offering. Johnny and Foo followed him.

As Johnny stepped back from the table, someone else came up behind him. It was a worker from the factory, a grey-haired man perhaps sixty years old. He picked up a stick of incense and waved it, bowed, and placed it in the jar. Two more people came behind him.

Johnny started filming again. A long line of people was moving towards the table, patiently waiting in the cold to make the offering. The candles shone brighter in the gathering dusk.

Peter sat in his chair to one side, his head spinning with fatigue and medication. He watched the long line shuffling forward and imagined he could see people he knew among them. Eric the banker and Cynthia's brother Ronald. *So, the world will know the truth at last,* he thought. *The secret will be told.*

Light will be thrown on darkness, Bezalia said.

Perhaps those frustrated spirits will be laid to rest. But me, I'm very tired, Bezalia. I want to get back and rest.

Peter was seized suddenly by an intense longing for familiar and comfortable things. He was homesick for warm weather and clean streets, for efficient medical care and his mother's cooking. *I want to go back to the hotel. I want to get on our flight back to Singapore.*

Yes, Peter. It's time to go home.

Chapter Twenty-one

'Look, my daddy on the TV!' Russell shouted. The television screen next to Peter's hospital bed showed a grimy concrete yard, leafless trees, a table set with offerings and incense sticks, a line of people waiting their turn. 'Uncle Peter, that's you!' Wintry sunlight gleamed on the metal of the wheelchair, highlighting the dark features of its occupant, and showed the four Singaporeans leading the ceremony.

'My hair is a mess,' Katrina remarked mildly.

'I remember it was very cold that evening,' Lumy said.

Tony Li's documentary 'Feeding the Hungry Ghosts' had launched on a premier American channel three days ago. A media storm erupted. The global media rushed to fill their channels with commentaries on the famine, and archival footage. China protested. Singapore Television, realizing that four Singaporeans were at the heart of the furore, screened the documentary repeatedly.

Four copies of the videotape arrived by courier from Tony Li. Alex brought a TV set to the ward where Peter, five weeks after their return, was still recovering from the journey. That evening, his friends gathered around Peter's bed and watched the program yet again.

On screen, Pei Yi stepped up to the altar. A few words of introduction from the commentator, then closeup of her solid features, her hoarse voice chanting a litany of the lost. Bleak subtitles translated her long lament.

They stopped watching when the documentary went on to an interview with a well-known China scholar, talking about the history of the famine. Lumy passed around boxes of Christmas cookies

'Have some nice cookies, Russell! Cynthia, I know you like the brandy snaps from the hotel!'

'My favourite! I can eat anything now. Doctor is so happy that I'm starting to get back my weight,' Cynthia said. 'He still doesn't know why I got sick. I can't tell him my husband had some bad dreams about China! But I believe that what you did in China satisfied those Hungry Ghosts—so they let go of me.'

'Katrina, I thanked Khoon Huat, for letting you stay in China so long,' Lumy said. 'I told him you were such a help to me, I couldn't have done without you.'

'So that's why he has been so nice to me, even though I'm still catching up with the work I missed!'

'Singapore Television wants to interview us,' Peter said. 'We'd better decide what we're going to say.'

'No dreams!' Alex and Katrina said almost together. 'They will take us to the mental hospital,' Katrina added.

'Let's tell them we read that book, about Hungry Ghosts.' Peter said.

'You showed us the book, I made photo copies for all of us to read,' Alex said.

'It made my heart hurt, just looking at the pictures in the book,' said Lumy. 'And I wanted to go to China to try to console them, comfort them.'

'Yes. We went out of our own compassionate impulse—to relieve our own distress,' Peter said slowly. 'That's what we will say. Keep it simple. We won't talk about Cynthia's illness, we won't mention that other patients like Jason are also getting better.'

'They will really think we are crazy, if we say Cynthia and Jason were sick because of that old China famine,' Alex laughed. 'Let them try to solve the mystery—they will never, never think of any connection.'

'Well, what was the connection?' Katrina asked. 'Why did this famine-sickness strike here and now—so far from China, so many years after?'

'Are you asking me? How do I know?' Peter laughed. 'I asked Bezalia, but you know she's not into explanations! It seems to me—there's a pool of psychic agony that gathers when there has been so much suffering and injustice. It lingers in the spiritual atmosphere, lying in wait like a radioactive source or a hidden virus, and sometimes it leaks out and harms the human world.'

'I think you cured my sickness,' Cynthia said firmly.

'Did we really satisfy the Hungry Ghosts?' Katrina asked.

'It was Bezalia,' Lumy said. 'Do you remember the last night before we left Nanchiao? Did you see her then?'

'We never talked about this,' Katrina said, 'we were so excited about going to Chengshen, and meeting Tony Li—I don't know if you all saw what I saw.'

'I saw Bezalia standing tall above us,' Alex said, 'and the crowds of starving ghosts all around. And she scooped up handfuls of magic food from our room, and she flung it to them—*Be fed!* she said. *Be fed!*'

'Then the crowds disappeared,' Katrina recalled.

'That was not food she threw to them,' Lumy said. 'It was Love.'

For a moment, they all were silent. The power of that remembered moment held them, and it seemed Bezalia stood among them.

'We brought Bezalia to China,' Peter said. 'We were the bridge for her to enter. She brought Love to them, to the ghosts, to Pei Yi and the people at Chengshen. And now that the world knows about it, the stories will be retold, the compassion will continue to flow.'

'So—we really changed the world,' Katrina said, awed.

'We were changed too,' Peter said. 'Everything that happened on our travels, helped prepare us to be carriers of love.'

'Yes, I think Alex has changed,' Cynthia said shyly. 'He's so good to me and Russell, every day.'

'Um. Ah,' Alex said almost blushing. 'Well, about this interview—we tell them we all read a book and got excited about going to China.'

'Tell them about Pei Yi,' Katrina said. 'Tony Li didn't put it into the show. Lumy, you know her story, you tell the reporters how her parents sold her when they all were starving. I bet they will be interested.'

'That's good,' Peter said. 'It puts the focus back on the people who were in the famine. All right, you all ready? Let's do Listening.' Cynthia and Russell joined them as they settled down. The ward staff, accustomed to the regular routine, came and went around the group. 'Listen to silence. Listen to your heart.'

* * *

By nine o'clock, the hospital corridors were empty. Peter lay quietly waiting for the last medication of the day.

Bezalia—I'm damn glad to be back in Singapore.

This is where you belong. This is where you have more work to do.

Yeah, well, Melissa and Lumy are running the Centre perfectly well without my help.

Laughter. *Let go of past achievements! You have tasks ahead that you have not dreamed of.*

Oh really? Peter said. *God's got future plans for me? As long as you're coming along for the ride . . .*

I will always be with you.

First, I gotta get off my back and out of this bed. Why is it taking me so damn long to recover? When am I going to get out of here?

But as always, he had to be content with not knowing, not having control.